BEAUTIFULLY BLIND

CANDIED CRUSH #14

CHARITY PARKERSON

—Warning: This book is intended for readers over the age of 18.

Copyright © 2021 Charity Parkerson
Editor: BZ Hercules & Consultants
ISBN: 978-1-946099-86-0
All rights reserved.

 Created with Vellum

INTRODUCTION

Koda needs a stubborn man. A man to teach him how to let someone love him. Felix has just what he needs.

Koda has a silent fame. While everyone knows his songs, no one knows his name. He has worked on backup vocals for the biggest names in music and on countless albums over the years. Koda is doing what he loves. His life is perfect... except it isn't. His fierce independence has become a wall, separating him from any chance at finding love. He needs help if he hopes to learn how to let people in. Luckily, he knows just who can help.

Since Felix leveled his life over a year ago,

nothing has been the same. Artists are severing their contracts with him, leaving him with way too much time on his hands. Felix never would have dreamed his private life would affect his work as a record producer this much. The only light in his day is Koda. Despite losing his sight at a young age, Koda has let nothing stop him. He's upbeat, successful, and he's driving Felix insane with longing.

When Koda asks Felix for a crazy favor, Felix sees his chance to finally have the man in his bed. Unfortunately, no one warned Felix he wouldn't want to leave... or that they've both been blind in more ways than one.

ONE

THE NOISE of the usual Saturday afternoon Bastien family get-together made Koda's ears throb. As much as he adored his huge family, they were some loud fuckers. It was a good thing he had bought his parents a house on ten acres a few years back. Otherwise, they would still get noise complaints every weekend from all their neighbors. They weren't known for their discipline.

Water splashed behind him where the kids and kid-like adults kept cannon-balling into the pool. A radio played in the distance, blasting eighties and nineties hair bands. Countless conversations buzzed around Koda, nearly sending him into overload. Most days, the ongoing busyness didn't faze him. Today, he felt like his brain itched. Koda wanted to get away. If only for a few hours, he craved silence.

"It's the usual fare. Hot dogs. Hamburgers. You know the drill. Would you like me to fix you a plate?"

Koda turned toward the sound of Zayn's voice at his question. Even though Koda had lost his sight at ten, he had been friends with Zayn's family since Koda was six. He recalled Zayn being in his late teens back when Koda could still see. Zayn had constantly tossed Koda in their old above-ground pool and chased him around the backyard. Back then, Zayn had been average height and scrawny. According to his mother, Zayn looked a lot different nowadays. In fact, she had been trying to convince Koda to go after the guy by bragging about Zayn's huge muscles, tattoos, and baby face. Koda wasn't interested in sharing his life with anyone. If he was, he might choose Zayn. Zayn was genuinely nice.

. . .

"No. Thank you. I was just standing here contemplating walking into traffic to make the noise stop."

A gorgeous and soft laugh caressed Koda's ears. "You should definitely let me fix you a hamburger instead. It would kill your mom if anything happened to you."

Koda knew that. He had amazing parents. "I guess I should eat something, then, since I doubt they'll let me leave."

A moment of silence passed. Koda could still feel Zayn standing there. "We could leave together. Our moms would love that, and we'd be free to find something quieter to do."

Zayn had his attention.

"Such as?"

. . .

"Honestly? I'd kind of like to just have you to myself."

Koda admired Zayn's bravery, and he was bored enough to bite. "To your place, it is. You should let our moms know we're going."

"On it."

As Koda waited for Zayn to return, he knew he was making a mistake. Like him, Zayn was here every Saturday. If they crossed any lines, they would be forced to pretend nothing happened for the rest of their lives. Not to mention, Koda really wasn't interested in Zayn. Zayn was great. The guy had a lot going for him. Anyone would be glad to have him. He had gotten rich by creating a crypto currency company way before it was cool. Now he spent most of his time on his body. He was a genuinely nice guy. On paper, Zayn seemed like the total package. But Koda was Koda. He didn't want to be tied down.

4

Nothing good came from love. Someone always got hurt. That wasn't something Koda wanted to bother with.

"Are you ready?"

All the good sense reasons he had just considered disappeared at the sound of Zayn's soothing voice. "Yep. Let's go." He was an idiot.

Working on Saturdays had been part of Felix's routine since two years into his marriage. Now that he was divorced and creeping toward forty, Felix could be honest with himself. He had created busy work for himself on Saturdays to avoid problems at home. Felix had been unhappy years before his ex-wife cheated, and then he had too.

In the past, unless there was a huge problem with a track, Felix had spent his Saturdays alone inside the recording studio. Here lately, he had developed a bad habit. He kept calling Koda in to help. Koda Bastien was the most popular backup singer used in today's hottest music. He had a voice to die for, but no desire to create his own music. Even though Koda wasn't tied to any particular studio or brand, most of his work was done right here. None of that had anything to do with why Felix couldn't stop begging Koda to join him on the weekends. Koda made Felix feel less alone. That was his only excuse for texting Koda again today.

Felix: *Are you interested in getting some work done with me today?*

The moment Felix hit send, the regret set in. It wasn't fair for Felix to constantly impose on Koda's life. He knew Koda spent Saturdays with his family. They were close and loved spending time together. Felix usually waited until closer to dark to increase the likelihood Koda would accept. Today, he was oddly desperate for company.

Koda: *I'm on my day.*

. . .

A laugh burst from Felix as he read Koda's text.

Felix: *I have no idea what being on your day means. Does that mean don't bug you on your day off?*

Koda: *Fucking speech to text hates me sometimes. I am on my way.*

For reasons Felix didn't want to look at too closely, he couldn't stop smiling at his phone. Koda always made him feel better. The ten minutes it took Koda to arrive felt like forever, even though he expected it would take much longer.

"Damn. You got here quick."

Koda flashed Felix a bright smile as he pushed through the front door of Felix's studio, Sommerland Music Group. He immediately shifted his sight cane to his left hand to keep it from getting crushed by the closing door. "A friend of mine was taking me home when you texted me. It didn't take long to change directions."

Felix's smile fell. "Am I ruining plans?"

Koda pulled a face that had Felix's gaze dropping to the man's full lips. Koda was really beautiful. "Actually, you saved me from myself. I was about to ruin a lifelong friendship by letting him fuck me." As Koda laughed at the confession, Felix's stomach twisted into knots. He fought hard to keep the unexpected jealousy from his voice.

"Oh, really? Do tell."

Koda made a dismissive gesture as he felt for the chair next to Felix and sat. "It was Zayn Tanaka. Our families have been friends since I was a kid. We were bored."

. . .

Felix's jaw dropped. "Wait. *The* Zayn Tanaka. The crypto currency guy?"

"Yep. That's him."

Damn. Felix honestly stood no chance with Koda. He had never met Zayn and had no clue what the guy looked like, but still. Felix had a slowly failing business, thanks to cheating on his wife and it blowing up in the news. Meanwhile, Koda was dark-haired and trim. His olive-colored skin was gorgeous and flawless. The most beautiful part of Koda was his mouth. He had a mouth that made men dream. Oddly, even though they had worked together for years, Felix hadn't really noticed Koda until a few months ago. Felix had gone through an ugly divorce and lost the man who had stolen his heart toward the end of his marriage. Koda had just sort of been there, and Felix found himself wanting more. Now he couldn't un-feel the growing emotions Koda stirred inside him. He was hopeless. Now Koda also had a billionaire after him. Felix would never be enough for someone like Koda.

· · ·

"What did you want to work on?"

At Koda's question, Felix scrambled to find something to keep Koda there. He hadn't had a real plan when he texted Koda. "Your latest contracts have started rolling in. Would you like to get a head start?"

Koda didn't answer right away. Instead, he sat facing Felix in silence, making Felix feel like Koda saw too much despite not being able to see at all. "Is that really what you want to do today?"

Felix swallowed. He knew Koda saw through him. "I guess. Never mind. You probably have a million things you'd rather be doing than being here with me. I shouldn't have asked you to come in." The more Felix rambled, the more he exposed of himself. "I was just here, and I like it when you're here too. It's too quiet here. So, you know…"

. . .

Koda took off his sunglasses and rubbed his eyes. It occurred to Felix that he had never seen Koda's eyes. Koda always kept them covered. He dropped his hand. The lightest green eyes Felix had ever seen stared at nothing.

"Goddamn."

A smile exploded across Koda's face. "What?"

Even though Koda couldn't see him, Felix shook his head. "Nothing. Never mind. You're beautiful. Fuck. I didn't mean to say that."

Koda snorted and put his sunglasses back on. "You should meet my family."

Felix blinked at the offhand remark. "Why? Do they have a penchant for collecting dumbass men?"

. . .

"Yes," Koda answered without missing a beat. "But that's beside the point. It's Saturday. You're bored, and they're not the least bit boring. Wouldn't you rather be at a pool party?"

Felix didn't need to think about it. "Yes, but I'm not dressed for a pool party."

"How are you dressed?"

Felix glanced down at himself as if he didn't know what he wore. "Jeans and a t-shirt. Should I change?"

"That depends on if you want to swim."

He really didn't. Not only did Felix have a pool he could use any time he liked, he also didn't relish going to a stranger's house and making himself at home. Instead of saying that, he went with the basics. "Not really."

. . .

"Great." Koda stood. "Let's go, then. If you need some noise in your life, my family has it to give."

With a sigh, Felix stood. He opened the front door for Koda and then locked it behind them. Koda stood quietly, waiting. Once he was ready, Felix set his hand on the small of Koda's back. "My car is this way."

As usual for Koda, his face lit—like he found everything more exciting than everyone else. "I've never been in your car. What do you drive?"

Felix had to bite his lip for a second. Koda was a completely unique soul. Felix felt good in his company. "It's a Bentley."

"What color is it?"

"Blue."

. . .

Koda nodded. "Blue like the sky or blue like blueberries?"

"Somewhere in between," Felix answered as he opened the door. "At what age did you lose your sight?" He had never asked since he thought it was rude, but it was obvious Koda hadn't always been blind.

Koda felt his way into the car. "Ten. Brain tumor," Koda said before Felix could ask.

Felix leaned on the door for a second and eyed Koda. He realized he wanted all of Koda's stories. "Have you ever seen a blue lobster?"

Koda's face lit. "Yes."

"That's what color my car is," Felix said as he shut the door. He rushed to the driver's side, hoping not to miss a second with Koda. As he slipped behind the wheel, he caught Koda stroking the seats.

"The leather is soft."

Felix started the car and took a steadying breath. Koda was tactile. Felix wanted to let Koda feel of his body. He needed to shut down those thoughts. No good could come of letting them take root.

"It also smells like you."

A chuckle stuck in Felix's throat. "I feel like that can't be good."

Koda's face turned his way. "Why? I've always thought you smell delicious."

Felix put the car in reverse by force of will alone. "I'm pretty sure I warned you once not to be nice to me." Felix knew he had. Months ago, when he had been at his lowest, Felix had told Koda he was like an abused dog. If Koda was nice to him, he would fall in love. Felix wasn't sure either of them wanted that.

"Just drive. I'll look after my safety. You look at the road."

With a shake of his head, Felix backed from his parking space. Spending the day with Koda outside the studio was likely a bad idea. He didn't plan to stop. "Where am I headed?"

"43652 Theodore Lane."

Felix did a double take. "And that's your parents' address?"

Koda nodded.

. . .

A laugh burst from Felix. "I live three houses down from there."

A smile exploded across Koda's face. "Ha. We live in a much smaller world than we thought."

"Apparently."

Felix headed toward his neighborhood. They made small talk all the way to their destination. With each easy word that passed between them, Felix's shoulders relaxed a little more. Even though he had always known they were friends, Felix felt even closer to Koda today. As he turned up the long and winding driveway, Felix focused on finding a place to park. Cars lined both sides of the driveway. Everything from a thirty-year-old Buick to a brand-new Aston Martin packed the front yard. He finally spotted an empty spot between two cars and pulled in.

"Wow. Who are all these people?"

. . .

"Mostly family," Koda said, taking off his seat belt. "Some are people my mom used to work with at her old manufacturing job. They were like a second family to her. To us too, I suppose, since we always spent weekends together. That's how I know Zayn. Our moms worked together."

"Now I'm sure neither have to work thanks to their wealthy sons."

"The circle of life," Koda said with a laugh as he exited the car.

Felix climbed out too and circled the car. He waited for Koda. Koda always walked with the confidence of a man with no sight issues. Sometimes, Felix forgot Koda couldn't see. Side by side, they headed for the door. Felix eyed the house. It was big, but not gigantic. He could hear children laughing and music playing. As they neared the front steps, Felix caught himself setting his hand on the small of Koda's back again. Koda slowed and used his stick to find the stairs.

Before they reached the front door, it opened. A brunette stood waiting with a huge grin. "Koda, baby. Didn't you leave here with a different man?"

"Yes," Koda said. His smile didn't hold an ounce of shame as he leaned in and kissed the woman who was a mirror image of him. "But you know I'm a whore. This is Felix. Felix, this is my mom, Elena."

Elena released Koda and hugged Felix. "Ah, *si*. The record producer. We've heard about you. It's so nice to finally meet you."

Felix wondered what they had heard. Probably nothing good. "It's nice to meet you too. I apologize for crashing your party. Blame Koda."

. . .

"I always do," Elena said with a laugh. She patted his chest. "But in this case, we love party crashers. This is an Italian family. We're big, loud, and nosy as fuck, so be prepared."

Felix couldn't stop smiling. Koda had been right. This was exactly what he needed. Unfortunately, Elena didn't stop there. She grabbed his hand and dragged him through the living room and into the kitchen. He didn't have time to take in the modern light-colored furniture, but the place smelled good— like home-cooked food. "Now tell me everything. How long have you been dating my son? Did you steal him from Zayn? You look to be Zayn's age. Can you afford to take care of my baby?"

Koda snorted behind them. "Your baby can take care of himself."

Elena made a dismissive gesture as if Koda could see everything. "Yeah, yeah. I know, but you deserve to be spoiled too. You shouldn't have to carry the relationship."

. . .

Felix couldn't help but to agree. "He really deserves to have someone buying him nice things, but we just work together."

"And we're fucking," Koda said, making heat explode across Felix's face.

"We're really not."

Elena swatted Felix's arm. "I know. My son is the jokester. He likes to try to scandalize me, but little does he know that I'll get to Hell before him and they'll welcome me with open arms." She lowered her voice to a fake whisper. "His hoe phase has nothing on mine."

Felix had never been more thankful Koda couldn't see, because Felix knew he was visibly dying.

. . .

"Let me grab you a drink."

As Elena turned away to grab him a beer from the fridge, Koda pressed his lips to Felix's ear. "I can feel your mortification. It feeds me."

Koda's hot breath brushing his ear had Felix turning his head. His mood instantly shifted with Koda so close. Hunger washed over him like a tidal wave. Their lips were only inches away. All Felix had to do was lean a hair closer and claim Koda's lips. He could ruin their friendship in a matter of seconds.

Koda's smile slipped away. His expression turned sexy as hell, making Felix's lust skyrocket. "Maybe embarrassment isn't what I'm feeling after all."

Before Felix responded and humiliated himself, Koda took a step back, and Elena handed him a beer. "I still have guests out back, so I'm going to leave you boys alone. Koda can keep you entertained."

· · ·

"I'm sure." The words were past Felix's lips before he realized what he said. He didn't take them back. Felix wanted to be distracted, and he was willing to bet there was a flat surface under this roof that would work for just that purpose. Fuck. He needed to get his life together.

———

Koda couldn't stop smiling. Dealing with Felix's problems was exactly the distraction Koda needed. The party was every bit as loud as it had been when he left, but Koda didn't feel suffocated by the noise anymore. He swore he could feel Felix's mood constantly shifting. Koda wanted to make it worse. He liked the chaos of Felix. There wasn't a doubt in Koda's mind that Felix would be explosive as hell in bed. All that pent-up emotion would blow up all over Koda one of these days. Koda couldn't wait.

"I'd offer you a tour, but I'm blind."

. . .

Felix snorted—like Koda made him choke on his beer. "It's fine. I'm sure your mom doesn't want me poking through her house anyway."

Koda shrugged. "There's probably a hundred people here. I doubt she cares. Do you want to join the party?"

"Sure."

At Felix's flippant tone, Koda snagged his arm and headed for the back door. As he wrapped his fingers around Felix's bicep, Koda couldn't stop himself from pushing up Felix's sleeve and going for bare skin. He stroked. Koda wondered if it made him weird that he much preferred the way Felix's arm felt compared to Zayn's. Zayn was a bodybuilder. No doubt people fawned over his hard body. Koda knew his mom did. But Koda liked the way Felix felt. He felt like Koda's type. Koda hoped his family didn't scare Felix away. They weren't exactly subtle, and some of them were downright mean. Koda wanted Felix to stick around.

. . .

The moment they stepped outside, Koda lost Felix. People engulfed them and introduced themselves. Felix got pulled away and Koda's mom snagged his waist.

"Come sit with me, baby. I want to know what happened with Zayn. You weren't gone but a few minutes and then you reappeared with this guy. Not that I'm complaining. He is fine. I mean F.I.N.E. Fine."

Koda couldn't stop smiling. "Really? Describe him to me." While Koda liked Felix for who he was and not his appearance, he had to admit he was curious. He knew his mom wouldn't hold back.

Elena held tight to his arm as they sat side by side in lawn chairs. "He's got messy brown hair—like stylish messy, as if he runs his fingers through it a lot, but it was cut to handle that. His eyes are light blue—like the sky, and he's covered in tattoos. I mean full sleeves and even his hands. If I didn't know he was a record producer, I would think he was some famous metal singer or something. He looks like a bad boy." His mom made a noise—like she found something curious. "He also can't take his eyes off you. Your uncle Karl has him cornered—no doubt asking how much money he makes, but he hasn't stopped staring at you. Whew. I don't know how you swapped Zayn for this one, but I don't blame you. This one has heat in his eyes. He wants you something fierce."

Koda fought the urge to press his hand against his stomach to quell the butterflies. "He texted me right after I left the party, wanting to work. I had Zayn drop me off at the studio and then I convinced Felix being here would be better than working." Koda hesitated. He had to be honest. "Mostly, I just wanted you to meet him."

Silence met his confession. After a moment, Elena squeezed his knee. "I know I'm always bugging you to give Zayn a chance, but I think this one is a better fit for you. I don't think Zayn will ever want more than to take you to bed. More than anything, I want you settled. This one has a hunger in his eyes. He wants you, and I'm not talking about that cute booty I created. I'm sure he wants that too, but that's not what I'm seeing right now. Felix has a matured desire. He wants all of you."

Koda nodded as his mom spoke. There was a knot in his throat. Koda wasn't scared of much, but he was terrified of love. Sex was something he understood. It was uncomplicated. A real relationship had the power to break him. No one other than his family had claimed to love him before. The idea of it shook Koda to his bones. Koda wasn't sure he cared to experience that, but he liked knowing Felix wanted him. It was a conundrum.

"Ope. Here he comes. Let me know how it goes."

His mom slipped away.

Koda held his breath, waiting as they exchanged a few pleasantries. Then Felix filled his mom's seat.

Koda found himself leaning Felix's way and latching on to Felix's arm with no real plan.

Felix leaned his way too. The surrounding noise disappeared. It felt like they were alone. "I like your family. They love you."

A smile tugged at the corners of Koda's mouth. "You gathered all that in the short time you were gone?"

"I'm intuitive. Plus, your uncle demanded to know my net worth to ensure I can buy you pretty things. When I hedged, he whipped out his phone and Googled me. Apparently, according to 'the Wiki,' I'm worth three hundred million."

Koda bit the inside of his cheek. He tried really hard. The Italian nosiness won. "Are you worth three hundred million?" It didn't really matter to him how much money Felix had, but that was a lot.

. . .

A sexy chuckle caressed Koda's ears. "I guess that depends on who you ask: Wiki or my ex-wife's lawyers. They tried to take me for half of five hundred million."

Koda's smile fell at the reminder of an ex-wife. He had known Felix for years. Koda had been there when Felix's ex-wife Megan had cheated and when Felix had fallen for one of his clients' twin. He had been there when Felix had gotten his heart broken by the twin, and when Megan had dragged him through the mud. Felix had remained mostly silent throughout. He had suffered alone.

"Sorry. I shouldn't have brought up Megan."

At Felix's claim, Koda realized he had been quiet for too long. "No. I'm your friend. You can talk to me about whatever you want. I want you to talk to me."

· · ·

Felix leaned even closer. Koda squeezed his arm a little tighter. Felix's voice turned sultry. "Am I your friend?"

Koda didn't know how to respond. The obvious answer was yes, but also no. Koda didn't want to be friends. He wanted to be more, but he didn't know how much more. Felix made him a little crazy.

"Um. There's some dude built like a bull bearing down on us, looking like he wants to kick my ass."

At Felix's words, Koda blinked, coming back to reality. "Is it an Asian guy with tattoos and a baby face?"

"Yep."

"Fuck. That's Zayn."

. . .

"May I speak to you alone?" The barked words floated down from above him.

Koda pasted on a bright smile at Zayn's dark tone, hoping to pretend it was just another day. "Of course." He shifted to his feet and Zayn grabbed his hand to help. Koda fought the urge to yank his hand away. He fucking hated being treated like he couldn't do things on his own. Since he had convinced Zayn to abandon their plans to have sex and to drop him off to hang out with another dude, Koda needed to be a little more passive. Now wasn't the time to assert his independence.

Zayn didn't speak until they were in the house. The moment they were closed inside the mudroom, Zayn stood too close. "What the fuck is going on? I left you at the studio so you could work. Then I get a call from my mom saying you're right back here with a date."

Koda stroked Zayn's chest, because he knew Zayn would let him. Damn. It was hard. "I'm not on a date. Felix is my record producer. He wanted to get started on some upcoming album work I have scheduled, but you had already gotten me out of the mood to work. So I convinced him to come meet the family instead."

He felt Zayn relax. "Oh. I'm sorry. It's just you two looked pretty cozy when I walked in."

It was hard to keep smiling. Koda felt like an ass. This was exactly why he had spent so much time avoiding his mom's matchmaking. No good could come of being with Zayn. Their families were too close, and Koda didn't want to settle down... mostly, he didn't want to settle. "Felix has been my producer for twelve years. He's my friend."

"Oh." Despite the sheepishness in Zayn's voice, Koda didn't relax. He didn't feel entirely safe being alone with Zayn. Zayn was too big. Between Zayn's size and Koda's lack of sight, Koda was at too much of a disadvantage. Zayn stroked Koda's cheek. Koda flinched. He hadn't expected Zayn to touch him. "I guess I've ruined things now."

Koda didn't respond. He didn't want to lead Zayn on.

Zayn took a step back and took a deep breath before releasing it. It was a loud sound in the otherwise quiet mudroom. "Tell your friend I'm sorry for being rude. Maybe by next Saturday you'll forgive me, and we can try again."

"There's nothing to forgive," Koda said automatically. "This was just a misunderstanding. We've known each other too long to make a big deal of anything." He hoped Zayn understood his double meaning. Koda didn't want there to be any anger between them, but he didn't want more either. Zayn wasn't the one for him.

"Of course. I'm going to sneak out the front door. Enjoy the party."

· · ·

Before Koda responded, Zayn was back in his space. His lips brushed the corner of Koda's mouth. He didn't back away. Zayn lingered, as if waiting for Koda to turn his head and make the next move. Koda held still.

Zayn finally took a step back. "See you soon."

Koda had no idea how long he stood there once he was alone. Most days, Koda was fine with himself and the life he had been given. Some days, like today, Koda didn't like himself very much.

"Are you okay?"

Koda's self-hatred ebbed as Felix's hand slid across the small of his back. Still, Koda spoke his thoughts despite his self-loathing disappearing at Felix's touch. "I don't know why I'm like this."

. . .

"How do you mean?" Felix kept finding ways to touch Koda. His caresses kept the confessions rolling.

"Like with Zayn. I don't want him. Not really. Why did I lead him to believe—even for a minute—that I do? In fact, if you hadn't texted me today, I'd probably be in his bed right now, wrecking a lifelong friendship between our families. I just don't understand why I'm so cold and self-destructive."

A soft chuckle stroked his ears. Felix rubbed Koda's hand between his. "Do you really think I'm the person to ask? I fuck up everything outside of my job, because I always feel too much."

"Well, I don't feel enough." Even Koda heard the petulance in his voice. He didn't want to turn bitter.

Felix took a step closer. Koda could feel the heat from Felix's body. Felix's hands landed on Koda's hips, freeing Koda to set his palms on Felix's chest. It was nice. He didn't feel intimidated the way he had with Zayn.

"What do you think would happen if we pitted my overabundance of emotions against your lack of caring?"

Despite the seriousness of their discussion, a smile touched Koda's lips. "I'd probably swallow you whole in my cavern of bullshit."

Felix shuffled even closer. Their bodies nearly touched. Koda wanted it to happen. "Or I'd fill you up until you choked on my neediness."

God. Koda wanted to choke. "Try me. I bet you can't change me."

"Deal."

· · ·

Koda blinked, coming back to reality. "What?"

"Do you want to tell your mom or should I?"

Koda's confusion grew by the second. "Tell her what?"

"That we're dating," Felix said, sounding triumphant as hell.

"Wait..."

The final inch disappeared between them while Koda still tried to finish his thoughts. Everything flew from his head as Felix's lips touched his. Felix didn't wait for permission the way Zayn had. He bit Koda's bottom lip, demanding to be let in. Koda felt the shift in power. Felix was in control. His kiss was sexy as fuck. It was carnal. Felix held Koda's face and stole his will. By the time Felix pulled away, Koda knew he had lost, but he still tried to fight.

. . .

"I've never exclusively dated anyone."

"Well, you are now."

Koda wanted to argue, but no words came. Instead, he found himself in Felix's arms again. He couldn't say he hadn't been the one to pull Felix toward him. Fuck his life. They were dating.

TWO

SINCE THEY HAD SNEAKED out without telling anyone goodbye last night, Koda had escaped telling his mom he had a boyfriend. Unfortunately, Koda hadn't been able to slip away from his thoughts. Felix had driven him home. The ride had been a silent one, with Koda trapped in his thoughts. Then Felix had insisted on walking Koda to his door. His first thought had been to use the opportunity to end this game. Instead, Koda had found himself backed against his front door in a heated exchange that had him begging Felix to fuck him. That hadn't happened either. Felix had left him at the door, panting, hard as a rock, and with the promise of seeing him today. The night had been a long one.

· · ·

Koda had swung wildly all night between breaking things off before he got hurt and seeing where this went. By the time Felix arrived at his door to spend the day with him, Koda's mind was set. He didn't want a boyfriend. He opened the door, definite in that decision. Then Felix was there.

Koda forgot his plan. "Hey."

"Hey back," Felix said, overcoming him. Koda welcomed him with open arms as Felix's mouth covered his. Damn. He smelled good and tasted even better. Koda didn't understand why they always came together so hot and heavy. They had known each other for years. How had they ignored each other before now?

Felix backed away a hair and tried speaking between kisses. "I'm sorry. I didn't plan to fall on you like this. Mhmm." He openly fought to regain control while stealing another kiss. "I'm taking you on a proper date. I'm stopping." He pushed away from Koda as if he had to force himself to stop kissing him. He could hear Felix panting. It was empowering as hell. "You're not wearing your sunglasses."

Koda glanced around, as if he could really see where he left them. His stomach muscles clenched with dread. The lust immediately disappeared. "Yeah. Sorry about that. I should find those."

Felix grabbed his chin and stole another kiss. "Why? You have gorgeous eyes. I like staring at them."

One of Koda's insecurities melted away at Felix's confession. "I've been told I'm unnerving when I look at people. You know, since I'm not really seeing anything beyond shadows."

"Huh," Felix said, sounding stumped. "Sounds like one of those bullshit things men do to make you feel like less, so they feel like more, to me. You should leave them off."

. . .

Koda wasn't sure he was ready for that leap. He would leave them off for Felix, but he would keep them nearby just in case he felt self-conscious. "Where are we going?"

"On my boat. So you should change and maybe grab a bag."

Koda didn't react right away. He didn't have many insecurities about being blind, but boats were one of them. "Um, so I don't really..." He thought better of his confession. The only thing Koda disliked more than the idea of being trapped alone in the middle of the ocean without even his sight to help him was anyone knowing his insecurities. "Okay. Give me a few." He paused. "What are you wearing for reference?"

"Swim trunks and a tank top."

Koda dipped his chin and headed for his bedroom. This was not how he had planned to spend his day.

Not that he would complain, because that wasn't him. He also knew he could say no. Felix wouldn't force him to go, but people didn't offer to take him places very often. Koda felt of his clothes, found what he was looking for, and changed. He also packed an overnight bag because he would not be a poor sport about this. Koda could do anything anyone else could do. That included dating a sexy music producer. A smile exploded across Koda's face. His mom had assured him of both things—he could do anything, and Felix was sexy. Koda fought a laugh. He was too positive for his own good sometimes. He found humor in everything.

Koda headed back out to the living room.

"You're smiling."

Fuck. Koda forgot to hide his ridiculousness sometimes. "Yeah. You're here."

. . .

Felix didn't respond right away. When he did, he had a hint of something unnamed in his voice. "Do you shop for yourself?"

Koda shifted uncomfortably. He didn't know how he looked. Usually, he didn't even think about it. "Yeah, but my mom always goes with me so I don't buy dumb-looking shit. Why?" As the words left his mouth, Koda's smile grew. His mom picked out his clothes and his men. He was a loser.

"I'll have to thank her. You look sexy as fuck."

An unexpected laugh burst from Koda. He wasn't doing a good job at keeping his inner weirdo hidden today. "Yeah. She'd definitely be the person to thank. She's responsible for the entire package, including me."

Felix drew an audible breath. "Damn."

. . .

Butterflies stirred in Koda's stomach. With a single word from Felix, Koda felt closer to getting fucked than he had after hours of making out in the past. Every single thought of wiggling out of this relationship disappeared. He had to know what it was like to be underneath Felix. Koda bet money it would be without compare.

No matter how hard Felix tried, he couldn't stop looking at Koda. He didn't know how to explain it. There was nothing special about Koda's outfit. Maybe it was the confidence he exuded. Koda carried himself like a man who knew his worth. Felix wanted to be close to him. After they reached Felix's yacht, Koda's demeanor changed. He didn't move with the same surety as usual. It wasn't until they were onboard and miles from shore that Felix realized his mistake. He truly had put Koda in a painful position. Koda couldn't see, yet he had to stay upright on a moving boat. His features were pinched. Felix regretted choosing this outing. The last thing he wanted was to make Koda feel unsafe with him.

· · ·

"I guess I should've taken us on a cliche date. It didn't occur to me you would be this uncomfortable."

Koda flashed Felix a tight smile. "It's fine. I'm just feeling a little sick."

Fuck. Felix had such high hopes for this date, but it wasn't going well. More often than he liked, Felix was a fucking moron. "You should sit." Felix led Koda to the couch and out of the heat. The craft wasn't huge. Felix needed something he could handle alone. But the yacht still had a galley, living room, full bathroom, and bedroom. Once Felix had Koda settled, he grabbed Koda a bottle of water and some anti-nausea pills. "Here. Take these. It should help. I'm sorry I didn't think this through."

Koda snagged Felix's shirt before he could get away and hauled him in for a kiss. "Don't apologize. I love that you treat me like I have no limits."

. . .

A chuckle rose in Felix's throat. "As far as I've seen, you don't. Seasickness isn't a limitation. It's a simple fix. If we decide to do this again, you can take something in advance and skip this part."

Koda swallowed the pills and then clasped his head. Panic raced through Felix when Koda leaned over and put his head between his knees. They hadn't been out for long at all. Felix felt like shit. Sometimes, he felt like he couldn't do anything right.

"Do you think it would help if you did the whole lying down with one foot on the floor thing? You know, like when you're drunk, and the room starts spinning."

Koda nodded. He reached for Felix for help standing, making Felix realize how bad he truly felt. Koda did not like for people to help him. Felix let Koda choose how much weight he wanted to lean on Felix as he led him to the bed. Koda sprawled out with both feet on the floor and draped his arm over his eyes.

. . .

"Just give me a few minutes to adjust. I'm not used to the floor moving beneath my feet."

Felix sat next to him. Despite Koda's sickness, Felix liked staring at him. "Take your time. If you want, I can take us back in. There's no reason for you to suffer. We could get some food delivered and be lazy the rest of the day."

A sexy smile curved Koda's lips. "It's cool. I'm just getting my bearings."

Felix turned sideways and sat cross-legged while staring at Koda. He was fine to sit there until Koda felt better or wanted to leave. "I know this isn't going well, but thank you for not shutting the door in my face earlier."

Koda still looked a little green, but he kept up his end of the conversation. "Well, I mean, according to you, we're a couple now. That means I let you in when you stop by."

A dry laugh fell from Felix's lips before he could call it back. "Don't pretend like you didn't spend all night trying to figure out how to dump me."

A humorless smile touched Koda's lips. "Don't pretend like you don't know why I don't trust anyone enough to date them."

That hurt. Felix had cheated one time in his life. Once. No one understood him, and maybe he didn't deserve to have a reason for what he had done. Maybe there was no good reason. He had been wrong, and now he would never deserve trust again.

Felix moved away and stood. "I should take us back to shore. There's no way you can stay out here all night."

. . .

"Don't do that."

Felix squeezed his eyes shut but kept his voice as light as possible. "Don't do what? Try to take care of you?"

Koda dropped his arm. His expression was serious. It was obvious he wouldn't let Felix blow this off. "That wasn't a shot at you. You know I'm not like everyone else. I was around, hanging in the background when Megan cheated. You never noticed me, but I was there for how it broke you. You went from trying to sound happy all the time to not even bothering anymore. I was there when you fell for Cade, and I was there when he broke your heart. No one notices me, but I've been here the whole time. I know you're not a cheat at heart. But I also know I'm not anyone's first choice. I don't want to start believing that I am. It has nothing to do with your past or you at all. In the eyes of everyone in this town, I am imperfect and... something to keep hidden, I suppose. I'm a guilty desire. A fetish. It's not your fault I don't know how to let anyone in. That's what I meant by me not trusting anyone's motives. It's nothing to do with you."

As someone whose name was complete shit in every L.A. circle, Felix understood what it cost Koda to make that admission. People in this town expected perfection. That was why Koda deserved to hear the truth. Koda was not a fetish or secret to him. "I knew I was in love with Megan by our third date. When she married me, I thought I had won the lottery. Then she wanted kids, and we struggled. No matter what we tried, it didn't happen for us. That was why the happiness disappeared. At first, she hurt, and then she got mad. When I found out she had been sleeping with someone else, it broke me." Felix hated having to tell this story, but he also had been dying from not sharing it with anyone. The words kept flowing. "Once it was my turn to hurt and turn bitter, I could see how much she hated me. I understood how it fed her to watch me suffer. She blamed me for stealing years of her life that she could've spent with someone capable of having kids. Then Cade thrust light into my life when I had nothing left to keep me going." Felix ran his fingers through his hair and scrubbed at his scalp. He knew he sounded like a terrible person, but he didn't stop. Koda deserved to know the real Felix. "I've made a lot of bad choices while trying to stay alive, and you're right. You've always been there in the background and I didn't notice. But that's not because I think you're imperfect; it's because I'm flawed in every way. I know you don't have any reason to trust that I want you for you and as you are, but I'm still asking you to give me a chance. I know I can care about you like no one else ever has. If that means taking you home so you don't have to suffer on this boat, then that's what I'm doing."

Koda didn't respond right away. When Felix was ready to turn away to take Koda home, Koda patted the bed beside him. "Sit back down, please. I'm not ready to give up yet."

An unexpected smile snapped to Felix's lips. He didn't know if Koda wasn't ready to give up on the boat ride or him yet. Either way, Felix was happy to oblige. "You're so stubborn." Even as he made the claim, Felix reclaimed his seat at Koda's side.

· · ·

Koda shrugged. "I can't let this beat me. Let's just talk some more. I can't give up yet."

Felix took Koda's hand and held it between his. "I won't let anything happen to you, but you're picking our next date."

A laugh burst from Koda. "Fair enough."

Felix couldn't stop smiling. He would sit there as long as Koda needed. Koda planned to give him a shot. Felix would make sure Koda never regretted it.

THREE

AFTER GETTING LEFT at his front door unmolested again, Koda decided he needed to take control. He also needed help. That was why he had a hot towel covering his face while his mom worked on his nails. Of course, that meant he had been forced to admit Felix was more than a friend. His mom was here for it.

"By the time I'm finished with you, you'll have men falling over themselves to get to you. Of course, they already do that."

. . .

"I just don't want to look dumb like I did this weekend."

Elena removed the towel. "I can't hear you through this thing."

Koda tried again. "I just don't want to look dumb like I did this weekend. Who gets sick on their first official date? I feel like an idiot."

Elena snorted. "From the way you talked, it sounds to me like Felix feels terrible for taking you out on that boat. I'm sure he doesn't think you looked like an idiot."

"Why are you scowling? I can feel you scowling." Koda always knew when his mom was angry. He could feel the heat radiating from her.

At his question, he swore the air lightened. Elena laughed. "It's nothing. I'm just being a mom.

Anything could've happened to you out on that boat. I know you can take care of yourself, but still."

Koda turned his face Elena's way. This was too important to let her have doubts. "You know I wouldn't have gone if I didn't trust Felix completely."

Elena rubbed his arm. "I know, baby. That's why I'm not lecturing you. I told you it's just the mom side of me. You're my baby. Half of my heart. If anything happened to you, I'd crawl in the hole with you." She sniffed. "Now. Felix took care of you and then didn't try anything while you were feeling bad. That makes him better than about seventy-five percent of the dating pool. Let's finish making you irresistible."

"I honestly don't know why I'm doing this. I've never cared how I look in the past."

Elena scoffed. "That's because you got my good genes. You don't have to try, but there's nothing wrong with pushing a man over the edge with how amazing you are when you put some effort into it."

For a few minutes, Koda stayed still and quiet, letting his mom pamper him. Unfortunately, they were too close for Koda to stop the confessions from flowing. "I guess what I really meant is, I've never cared about anyone enough to care what they think."

Elena went still. When she spoke, her tone didn't match the intensity he felt vibrating from her. "So you care about this guy."

Koda tried to be as nonchalant as possible. His mom could be pretty overwhelming when she wanted. If she knew too much about Felix, she would definitely butt in. "Yeah, I mean, we've known each other for several years. We're starting out on a foundation of friendship. That's not the same as anyone else I've dated."

"Honey, you haven't dated anyone."

. . .

A smile exploded across Koda's face. "I can't help it I got your independent personality."

Elena laughed. "And my sex drive."

"No," Koda cried while fighting back laughter.

"You're such an easy mark." The happiness in Elena's voice kept him smiling. He knew he had a ridiculously open relationship with his mom, but he was so thankful for it. Without her willingness to be more than just a mom to him, Koda's life would have been horribly dark and lonely. She was the one person he hadn't been able to shut out.

The humor disappeared from Elena's voice. "I wish I hadn't pressed so hard about Zayn and you. He's obviously always been way more interested than you are."

. . .

"And now there's a wrench in your friendship with his mom," Koda finished for her.

"Hmm, I don't know. I don't think Hana knows what she wants for Zayn. Well, that's not entirely true. She'd love it if he woke up tomorrow not gay, but that's not happening. You were her second choice, since it would be like keeping his secret with our group—like fewer people would know or something." Elena snorted. "As if no one can tell he's gay. He's pretty cocky. It'll take someone strong to pin him down. That wasn't my point, though. I wish I had seen what you really need isn't someone who matches your over-the-top level of confidence."

Koda fought the urge to admit he wasn't confident in the least when it came to Felix. "What do I need?"

Elena leaned close and kissed his cheek. "A nice guy," she said, wiping his cheek as if wiping away lipstick. "You won't settle until you have someone kind." She smacked his shoulder. "And stubborn.

59

Woo, are you're going to need a man that'll stick to you no matter what because you can be trying."

Despite Elena's claims, he couldn't stop laughing. He knew she was serious, but he couldn't take it to heart. Koda swiped at his eyes and sighed. "I love you. I don't know what I would do without you."

"I love you too, baby. Let's get this finished. Life won't solve itself today."

That was true. He wouldn't likely resolve every problem he faced with one chat. Koda felt better about life, though. He felt like he might not fail Felix immediately. However, next week might be a different story.

Felix swore he felt Koda come through the door before he saw him. He had known Koda was on the recording schedule for the day. Felix hadn't expected his immediate reaction to seeing Koda again. He hadn't seen Koda since he left Koda at his front door after their boat date. They had sent a few texts back and forth, but they hadn't made plans to see each other again. Now, as he watched Koda smile and speak to everyone as he stepped inside the studio, Felix found himself stricken anew by the overwhelming need to be in Koda's company.

Koda cared about people. He stopped and spoke to everyone. Koda asked the receptionist, Mike, about his dog that had recently eaten a poisonous plant. He listened as the guy who worked in editing talked about his kids. Koda knew all of their names. It hit Felix. Koda really had been right here all along. In the background. Never getting the attention he deserved. Felix wasn't sure he would forgive himself for that lapse.

Then Koda's face turned Felix's way, as if he knew Felix stood there watching him. A small smile touched Koda's sexy lips. Felix could barely breathe. He knew how those lips tasted. Felix wanted more. Koda wore a black button-down shirt with the sleeves rolled up to his elbows, and the top three or four buttons were undone. A pair of black pants molded to his skin, shaping his round ass to perfection. Felix's mouth was dry as the Sahara.

"Hey, Koda."

Something wicked crossed Koda's features. "Hey."

Felix had to take a breath. He wanted Koda... bad. "Do you mind if I talk to you for a second before you jump in the booth? I have a few things to go over with you. Last-second changes and whatnot."

Koda crossed the room. "Sure thing."

Felix inhaled Koda's scent as he passed. He smelled sweet yet spicy. Felix needed to taste him. He closed the door, shutting out the world. "Goddamn. You look sexy as fuck today."

. . .

Koda smirked. "I like to think I look that way every day, but thank you for noticing."

Felix couldn't stop himself from crowding Koda's space. "Let's do something after you finish up today."

"What would you like to do?"

You. Felix fought hard to keep that thought to himself. "Anything at all as long as we're together." He rubbed Koda's sides, drawing him closer. Felix couldn't tear his gaze away from Koda's face. "Is it strange that not seeing you for two days has been hell? I shouldn't miss you already, but I do."

"We should remedy that." Koda's hand came to rest on Felix's shoulder. He slid his hand up until he cupped Felix's jaw and his thumb caressed Felix's chin. A smile exploded across his face. "You have a slight dimple in your chin. Adorable."

.   .   .

It struck Felix. Koda had no idea what he looked like, yet he still let Felix touch him. It was humbling and flattering. He liked how that knowledge felt in his chest. "Is it okay if I kiss you?"

Koda's smile slipped away. His expression turned heated. He took a step closer. His body collided with Felix's. Before Felix could claim Koda's lips, Koda took charge. He opened his mouth over Felix's bottom lip and sucked. Felix's knees weakened. Everything about Koda turned him on. He had so much confidence. Koda possessed this unmatched surety that he was wanted by anyone he chose. It was sexy in a way Felix couldn't describe. Felix's body burned as Koda curled his tongue around Felix's and stroked.

Koda took a step back. "Let me get through my workload and we'll get out of here."

Felix nodded. He was dazed from Koda's kiss. All he could do was watch as Koda let himself out. He closed the door behind him. Felix stared at the closed door. A tiny whimper escaped him as he reached down and readjusted his erection. The last few months had been hell. His heart was set on Koda. No one else could satisfy him.

Felix tore his gaze away from the door and circled his desk. He dropped into his chair. While Felix didn't think taking Koda straight to bed was a good idea, he didn't know how much longer he could resist.

A light tap on the door pulled Felix from his thoughts. Hope surged in his chest that Koda had come back for more. "Yes?"

The door opened and Koda's mom poked her head in. "Hey there. I hope I'm not bothering you."

Felix shot to his feet. "No. Come in." He circled the desk again and met her halfway.

. . .

Elena hugged him and kissed his cheek before he knew it would happen. "Thanks for making time for me."

Even though Felix was confused, since it wasn't like they had an appointment, there was no way he would make Koda's mom feel unwelcome. "Have a seat. I always have time for you."

With a grateful smile, Elena claimed the chair across from his desk. Felix chose the one beside her rather than the one behind his desk. He didn't want to make her feel like she was at a business meeting.

Elena patted his arm. "I had so many guests this weekend, I don't feel like I got to properly meet you. Since I brought Koda in today, I thought I would pop in and try to do better."

Felix waved off her concerns. "Think nothing of it. I crashed your party. You didn't have to entertain me."

. . .

She flashed him a bright smile, and it hit Felix how much Koda looked like her. They had the same dark hair and green eyes. Their lips were shaped the same, and they smiled alike. He immediately warmed to her.

"Koda tells me you got him on a boat on Sunday."

Felix's smile slipped away. "Yeah. I wish I hadn't. Until we were out on the water, I didn't realize how terrified he was. I should've been more observant."

Elena nodded. "I'll admit, when I first heard, my stomach dropped. But he says you took good care of him, and he trusts you completely. He's always been an amazing judge of character, so I know I can trust you to take care of my baby."

"I would never let anything happen to him." Even Felix heard the vow in his tone.

. . .

Elena nodded, looking serious, as if she too understood how important Koda's existence was to Felix. "I'm glad to hear it. He's incredibly stubborn. He got that from his dad." A smile snapped to Felix's lips, but Elena wasn't finished. "You'll have to be a fighter to hang on to him. He's the most independent person I've ever met. But he needs love, even if he doesn't want to accept it. Hell, after he lost his sight, even I had to fight to keep him from shutting me out. He doesn't like to look weak. For whatever reason, he's convinced himself that loving anyone weakens him." That sounded like Koda to Felix. Elena shook her head. She looked at a loss. "Honestly, it's been frustrating as hell, watching him convince himself no one wants him for more than one night while knowing he's the one who pushes people away. From what I hear, you're pretty stubborn too. I think you're probably the only person who can actually win him."

There was so much pride in Felix's chest, he could barely breathe. He knew he should be slightly insulted she had heard stories about his mulishness, but no. She thought he could win Koda. That was exactly the confidence booster Felix needed. "I'm not going anywhere. He'll have to hire a tow truck to move me."

A bark of laughter burst from Elena. She slapped his knee. "Good. That's what I like to hear." She stood. "Now, I know you're a busy man, and you're likely to have tons of work to do. But I conned your receptionist into clearing your schedule for the next two days." Before Felix recovered from that high-handed announcement, Elena handed him a piece of paper. "I've made reservations for two at a bungalow in Santa Barbara for two nights. You also have dinner reservations. It's all on the itinerary and a champagne basket will be waiting in your room. Have fun." She pointed at him and her expression turned serious. "Whatever you do, do not tell Koda I was here, or that I had anything to do with this. You take the credit and it'll be our secret."

Felix didn't know how to react. He didn't know what to say. This was the oddest thing that had ever happened to him. "Thank you." The words popped out automatically, saving him in his moment of need.

· · ·

A bright smile lit Elena's face. She patted his cheek. "You're very welcome. Now make my son happy. Also, we'll be out of town this weekend. Ronaldo is taking me gambling in Vegas, so you don't have to worry about any family events for a while. Just go and relax."

Despite his shock, Felix recognized how amazing she was. Intrusive as hell, but amazing.

Felix stood and gave her another hug before walking her to the door. They exchanged some small talk before finally saying goodbye. Felix walked in a stunned haze back toward his office. The sight of Koda caught and held his attention before he made it. Felix leaned against the soundproof window and watched as Koda sang his heart out. Felix flipped the intercom on so he could listen to the passion in Koda's voice. He had no idea how long he stood there.

A movement at his side caught his attention. He glanced over to find Mike at his side, watching Koda too. A small smile lingered on Mike's lips. Felix almost said something about Mike getting conned into clearing his schedule, but he couldn't bring himself to complain. He didn't imagine Mike had stood much of a chance against Elena.

Mike glanced Felix's way. His smile grew. "He's crazy talented. I'll never understand why he doesn't want a contract of his own. He shouldn't be in the background."

Even as Felix nodded, he acknowledged the truth. Koda didn't want to put himself in a position where people would constantly bring up his blindness. That was exactly what would happen if he chose to be the face of the songs he sang. If Koda moved into the spotlight, no one would ever see him as anything more than his disability—like his voice was somehow less or more because of his eyes. They lived in an unfair world. Felix respected Koda's feelings on the matter.

. . .

The phone rang, pulling Mike away. Felix stayed put, unabashedly watching Koda work his magic. Elena was right. Felix was the right man for Koda. Koda would eventually try to keep him out. Felix had no intention of letting that happen. He had Koda now. There was no going back. Koda just hadn't realized it yet. He would.

FOUR

DESPITE HIS BEST efforts to hide his excitement, Koda was practically crawling around the passenger side of Felix's car. After finishing his work for the day, Koda had planned to close himself in Felix's office and seduce him. Instead, he found himself whisked away. First, Felix had taken him home and demanded Koda pack a bag for a few nights. From there, they had driven for what felt like forever. In truth, it had only been about two hours, including sitting in traffic. It was only Koda's excitement making it seem longer.

Felix left him alone in the car while he checked in to their room. Since Koda didn't know where they were, he waited for Felix to let him out of the car. The moment his car door opened, the sounds and smell of the ocean washed over Koda. Unlike their boating trip, this felt different. A smile exploded across Koda's face. He knew exactly where they were.

"Oh my god. You talked to my mother. There's no other way you knew Santa Barbara is my favorite place."

"Is it? I had no idea. We are in Santa Barbara, though."

Koda snorted at Felix's dodging. There was no way this was a coincidence. They might have known each other a long time, but there was no way Felix knew this was Koda's favorite place. He doubted this had simply happened.

"Let me guess. We have a bungalow on the beach."

· · ·

"Yep."

At Felix's response, another snort escaped Koda. His mom was such a meddler. "How long did Mom wait after I got in the booth to corner you?"

"Maybe five minutes."

Laughter burst from Koda at Felix's immediate response. Koda didn't care how the trip came about. He loved this place. It was one of the few places he could remember seeing before losing his sight. His parents brought him here every year as a child. It was the one big trip they saved for each summer.

"Let me grab our bags and we'll head inside."

Koda dutifully stood still until he heard the trunk close. Then he held out his hand. "Here. Hand me my bag and you can steer me in the right direction."

· · ·

Felix didn't argue. He simply passed Koda his bag, and that was one of the many reasons Koda adored him. Felix never treated him like a child. Together, they headed inside. Felix lightly held his elbow on the way to the door. Koda's cane hit a small step on the way inside and he followed its lead. Cool air washed over him as he stepped inside the bungalow. It smelled like every beach hotel ever. Soap and sand.

A soft and sexy chuckle rumbled from Felix.

A smile immediately snapped to Koda's lips. "What?"

Felix didn't leave him in suspense. "Your mom said she would have some champagne waiting for us. Not only are there three bottles, but there's also roses and chocolate-covered strawberries."

"She's not very subtle, is she?"

. . .

"I like her."

Felix's confession warmed Koda's heart. He knew his family could be overwhelming, but it was important to him that Felix like them. Koda didn't know why. It just was.

"Thank you for this." The words popped out, but Koda needed to say them.

Felix invaded his space. His palms slid across Koda's hips. "I'm not the one you should thank, but I wish I had thought of this."

Koda didn't back down. "I know this has Mom written all over it, but you still deserve the credit. Not everyone would let my mom do this. You could've said no."

"No. I couldn't." Felix's tone had turned sultry. Goosebumps rose on Koda's skin. "There's no way I could have or would have said no to being here with you. Tell me what you want to do first and I'm in. I haven't had a vacation in years."

"We should check the bed," Koda said without hesitation. He had wanted Felix too long. They were alone now. The bed was so close. Still, he tried to sound a little less desperate. "You know, because they're sometimes too hard." Damn. He didn't sound any less like a wanton.

Felix didn't call him on it. "You're probably right. The last time I stayed in a place like this, my back hurt for three weeks afterward. We should check." Felix led him toward the bed. At the edge, he guided Koda's hand to where he could leave his cane and find it later. After toeing off his shoes, Koda climbed onto the mattress and settled onto his back. The bed dipped beside him as Felix did the same. Elbow to elbow, they fell into silence. It was uncomfortable. For Koda, it was as if time held its breath, waiting. Their fingers linked. Koda wanted so much more. He couldn't take it any longer.

. . .

"Is it okay if I touch you?"

Felix didn't let him down. "Of course."

Even as Koda rolled to his knees, intent on doing what he wanted before Felix changed his mind, he still felt the need to explain. Koda straddled Felix's hips. "I'm always curious about people's features, but it's super rude to touch people. It's an issue." He moved slowly, so he wouldn't poke out Felix's eyes or anything. Koda gently stroked Felix's nose and cheekbones, taking in his every feature. "Mom tells me you're covered in tattoos."

Felix snagged Koda's waist and sat up. Clothes rustled and Felix settled back down. "I can help you with seeing those. Here." Felix took Koda's fingers and led them to his chest. "Right here, there's a skull wearing dark blue sunglasses with the sun setting in the reflection of the lenses." Felix traced the outline with Koda's fingers, showing him how big it was. He moved to his ribs. "Here I have some sheet music." He moved Koda's fingers along each note.

. . .

Excitement raced through Koda. "Wait. Do it again."

Felix obliged.

Koda read the music as Felix led. "It's Franz Liszt."

"Damn. You're good." Koda could hear the smile in Felix's voice. "He was the very first rockstar. I couldn't choose anything else."

Koda needed more. He wanted every detail. "What's next?" He didn't try hiding his excitement.

Felix moved Koda's hand to the opposite ribs. He used Koda's index finger to draw the word written there. Koda's forehead furrowed as Felix restarted the word, giving Koda time to figure it out for himself.

. . .

"Sinful?"

At Koda's inquiry, Felix hummed. "Mhmm. Yep. That's me. Well, that's me, according to my father. He was a youth pastor, and he hated everything I did."

Felix's choice in words confused Koda. "Was? Has he passed?"

Felix flattened Koda's palm against his chest and held it there. "Not as far as I know. My mom divorced him when I was sixteen after finding out he had been sleeping with all the teenage girls he was supposed to be counseling. I haven't seen him since."

Koda's heart dropped. He had such a great family... with a few exceptions. Sometimes he forgot other people weren't as lucky. "What about your mom?"

. . .

He felt Felix shrug. "She's around. We see each other on holidays, but that's about it. She's always busy traveling and whatnot. I'm always busy working."

Koda couldn't leave it alone. "What made you decide to get that tattoo? Surely you don't believe that's true."

"It is true," Felix said without missing a beat and surprising Koda. "Not only is it true, it's the best thing about me. I know he thought he was insulting me, but no. He considered my music choices too lustful and my bisexuality as going against God. I like who I am. I create songs that give people an escape. If that makes me sinful, then fuck yeah. That's who I am." The passion in Felix's voice had Koda smiling. Then Felix's voice turned sexy. "If being here with you makes me sinful, then I'm proud to wear the title."

Koda smiled. He had to lighten the situation. Sometimes Felix said things that got a little too intense for Koda. "What's that like? Being bisexual," he added, clarifying his question.

A laugh burst from Felix, making Koda's smile grow even larger. Felix toyed with Koda's fingers. "I don't really think about it, honestly. It's always been like, damn, he's hot, or wow, look at her. Truthfully, I've always been slightly more attracted to men than women, but it's a lot more intimidating being with a man."

Koda hadn't expected that. "How so?"

He felt Felix shrug again. "I don't know. Guys expect you to be perfect. They want you to look a certain way and be a certain way. If you're bisexual, they automatically assume you'll cheat with a woman. Yet they always want an open relationship so they can cheat with other men. Women are simpler. They just want someone who stays faithful and lets them eat what they want." Felix's voice turned sad. "Not that I've had a lot of luck with anyone of any sex staying faithful to me."

. . .

Damn. Koda completely understood Felix's hurt. Dating was like that. Everyone wanted perfection while never offering the same. Koda couldn't let Felix be sad. He intentionally turned up the brightness. "Well, things are different for you now, buddy. I don't give a fuck what you look like, because I can't fucking see you."

Felix's mood didn't lift. "What about the rest?"

Koda's smile slipped away. He didn't know if he would be any good at being in a relationship. But the idea of cheating or sharing made him sick, and he didn't want that. Plus, he hated that bullshit. Koda only wanted Felix. That fucking terrified him. "I don't see myself as the type to share or cheat, but—to be fair—I am the type to run."

Silence met his confession. After a moment, Felix released a tired-sounding sigh. "Well, that's legitimately depressing."

. . .

The more they talked, the more nervous Koda became. His stomach shook. Still, Koda wasn't ready to back down. He was too happy while straddling Felix's hips with Felix toying with his fingers. A wild idea struck. "You know how you chased Cade when you two broke up?"

"Wow. We're hitting all my best highlights today."

Koda ignored the sarcasm in Felix's voice. He had to run with this crazy plan before he changed his mind. "Be that intense with me."

Felix laughed. The sound died away when Koda didn't join in. "Wait. You're serious."

Even though it hadn't been a question, Koda nodded. "Just hear me out. I don't expect you to look perfect and I don't want an open relationship, but I can't promise I won't run. So don't let me."

. . .

"Koda…" Felix sounded like he planned to say no. "… I really don't want to look like a fool anymore."

Koda got it. He wasn't like Cade. Koda wasn't perfect. He wasn't worth chasing. "Oh. Okay. I just…" Koda didn't know how to finish that sentence. He thought Felix was serious about dating him, but he couldn't say that. He refused to look dumber than he already did. His pulse drummed in his ears. The panic he had avoided for a long time came racing back to the surface. Koda was hours from home and Felix had driven. This was a worst-case scenario for him. He was trapped with someone who didn't want him in a place too far to easily get home. Goddamn. This was why he didn't date. He was always at a disadvantage. How had he left himself get into this position?

"I don't think coming here was such a good idea." Koda tried climbing from the bed and almost fell.

. . .

In a flash, he found himself on his back. Felix settled between Koda's thighs. Even though Felix was on top, Koda didn't feel pinned. "Please don't go."

Koda's heart rate immediately slowed at Felix's quiet plea. He sounded genuinely hurt at the idea of Koda leaving.

"Okay."

Felix's lips lightly brushed Koda's. "Just stay." Felix punctuated the quietly spoken words with another light kiss. "I want you here." Felix sucked Koda's bottom lip. Every thought of leaving melted away. There was nowhere he would rather be right now. As Felix deepened their kiss, Koda forgot why he had been upset in the first place. This was all he wanted in the world. Koda might never move again.

No matter how hard Felix fought against his nature, he always lost. He was needy. Felix preferred being part of a pair. Single life wasn't for him. He had loved being a husband, even when things had first turned bad. Until the moment Megan cheated, he hadn't imagined getting divorced. So he could argue he wouldn't beg anyone to leave him, but—obviously—that wasn't true. He had chosen Koda. Now, he couldn't let him go. He would beg and chase. Koda was his now.

Felix poured all those feelings into their kiss. Truthfully, he was so upset at the idea of Koda leaving that it took a minute before his brain switched gears. It took Koda shoving his hand between their bodies and unbuttoning Felix's jeans before the lust took over.

Felix pulled away long enough to steal Koda's shirt. Then he was back, owning Koda's mouth. Their tongues stroked like they were desperate to touch. Felix couldn't stop moving against Koda, fucking him with their pants on. He couldn't get enough of the way their bare torsos felt against each other. He craved Koda. For months, he had been watching Koda, wanting him. Now he had Koda beneath him. It felt like a blessing. Still, he didn't want to take advantage.

.   .   .

"I can stop," Felix said as he moved to kissing Koda's neck. "I didn't plan this."

Koda slapped his hand against the headboard and moaned. Until that moment, Felix hadn't realized how aggressively he had been humping Koda. He didn't stop. Koda visibly strained toward release. Felix couldn't focus on anything else. Koda was shameless. It was obvious he was about to come in his expensive black pants, and Koda raced toward that fate. Felix couldn't tear his gaze away from the sight. He needed to watch. A loud cry tore from Koda. Felix lost his breath. Emotion washed over him. It was as if a million realizations hit at once. There was no one better than Koda. Felix would plead to stay with him. They had known each other for years. Since Koda was seventeen, to be exact, which should be weird, but it wasn't. Felix had watched him grow into the confident man beneath him. Maybe he hadn't noticed Koda until recently, but he saw Koda now. Felix would protect him with his life.

.   .   .

With his cock still begging for his turn at release, Felix softly kissed Koda's throat and rolled away. He headed for the bathroom. After finding a washcloth, he wet it with warm water and headed back to bed. Every step was almost painful in his lust. Before he reached Koda to clean him up, Koda rolled from the bed and stripped out of his pants and underwear. Felix stood frozen halfway to the bed. Koda was perfect. It was possible Felix saw him through his feelings and that made Koda ten times hotter, but Felix doubted that was the case. Another thought hit, rocking Felix on his heels. Koda couldn't see himself, and he couldn't see Felix. Yet he chose to be here. Felix's throat swelled. He wasn't worthy.

"Come here."

At Koda's demand, Felix forced himself out of his head. "I got you a washcloth."

Koda looked sexy and ready for more. His intensity had Felix's mouth going dry. "Set it aside. I don't need it yet."

. . .

A stuttered breath escaped Felix. He set the washcloth on the nightstand and closed the distance between them. The moment he was within striking distance, Koda snagged the waistband of Felix's jeans and underwear and shoved. Felix did his best to help Koda strip him, but Koda was in charge. Once he was nude, and before Felix could figure out Koda's next move, Koda was on his knees. Felix's dick was in Koda's mouth. Felix searched for anything to cling to, hoping to stay upright. There was nothing. He buried his fingers in Koda's hair instead. Then Koda swallowed him.

"Oh god." The words tore from Felix's throat as Koda's throat tightened around him. Even though Felix was completely incapable of thinking about anyone else, he knew he had never had a blow job this good. He was about to embarrass himself. There was no way he would last long. The pressure built. Sounds tore from Felix's throat he couldn't control. He tugged and pulled at Koda's hair, fucking Koda's mouth. Koda used both hands and his tongue to drive Felix mad. Every muscle in Felix's body tightened in anticipation. He felt the first spasm build. Koda tightened his fist around Felix's cock so hard that he stopped Felix from coming. A whimper escaped Felix.

Koda shot to his feet, denying Felix the orgasm he needed. "Get on the bed."

Felix scrambled to obey. He wanted to come. The moment he settled onto his back, Koda was there, between Felix's thighs and sucking him. The threat of orgasm was back. Felix's eyes burned as he fought not to blink against the sight of Koda bobbing on his dick. He dug his heels into the mattress and pushed against Koda's mouth. Felix wanted everything from Koda. This time, when the first spasm hit, Koda didn't stop him. When he blew, it felt like the orgasm he lost hit with this one, pulling multiple orgasms from him at once. That had never happened to Felix. His body shook and his moans bounced from the walls. Koda kept sucking, taking everything Felix could give him. Felix felt like he lost a part of himself. Despite the pleasure pulling at his eyelids, Felix still couldn't look away from Koda. He had never felt so free to watch every nuance of getting pleasured. The sight seared into his brain. Felix knew he would never touch himself again without seeing Koda on his cock.

Before Felix caught his breath, Koda rolled away and was on his feet. He had his cane and searched the room. Felix gasped for air, watching as Koda found the sink and washed his face. It was as if nothing happened between them. There were no kisses or whispered promises. Koda was done.

"We should find a place for dinner."

As Koda's words sank in, so too did his expression. He had closed his heart against Felix. Koda had wrapped himself in a protective coating so thick and fast that Felix could practically see his walls as a tangible thing. It hit Felix. No one cuddled Koda. They didn't stay and hold him. He didn't get aftercare or sweet kisses. People fucked him and left. Felix was in his feelings and couldn't take it.

. . .

"We will in a little while. First, come here."

Koda crossed the room. Felix sat up, set Koda's cane aside, and dragged Koda back onto the bed. He wrapped himself around Koda, hoping to break through the wall Koda erected. Koda wrapped his hands around the arm Felix draped over him, as if he didn't know where else to put his hands. Felix kissed Koda's ear and then his cheek, luring him in. Koda drew a ragged-sounding breath and turned his face Felix's way. Triumph rang through Felix's mind as their tongues met. He found himself back between Koda's thighs, but this time, it had nothing to do with sex. Felix just needed to be as close as he could get to Koda. Their nude bodies molded. Felix's heartbeat kissed Koda's chest, as if trying to touch Koda's heart. He held Koda as close as he could and settled in. They weren't going anywhere. Felix would make Koda feel him. There was more to them than desire. Felix wouldn't stop until Koda saw it too. Koda didn't need to protect his heart. Felix was here to steal it, and he would keep it safe. This was the start of something real.

FIVE

A TWO-DAY GETAWAY turned into seven. They simply hadn't wanted to leave. Felix kept clearing his schedule, and Koda kept letting him. They spent their days exploring the town and enjoying the beach. Their nights were spent touching and kissing. Oddly, Felix hadn't tried having sex with Koda. Koda was a little off balanced by that. He wondered if Felix wasn't a fan of penetrative sex with a man. Koda also wondered if they should talk about it, but they didn't.

It was their last day together. Koda tried hard to keep smiling while Felix drove him home. No doubt everything would change once they were back where everyone knew them. Felix wouldn't want everyone taking their pictures together. He likely wouldn't want to see Koda again. It was one thing to go to Koda's parents' house and out on Felix's boat. No one knew them when they went everywhere together in Santa Barbara. L.A. was different. People here would talk if they were seen holding hands. Koda didn't imagine Felix really wanted that. It was hard to keep smiling. Things wouldn't be the same here. Koda hadn't realized how much he wanted what Felix had given him this past week until he had it. Now Koda didn't want their connection to end.

"I know we just spent the entire week together," Felix said, cutting into Koda's growing depression. "But how do you feel about packing another bag and coming home with me? We could go out to dinner tonight and do whatever. I'm not ready to go back to sleeping alone."

Koda fought the urge to smile like an idiot. It was always like Felix could read his mind and cut through the bullshit it created. "I admit I was just sitting here thinking about how much I don't want to sleep alone tonight. But aren't you sick of me yet?"

Felix brought Koda's hand to his mouth. His lips brushed Koda's knuckles, making butterflies stir in Koda's stomach. "I don't think it's possible to tire of you."

"How can I resist that challenge?"

Felix chuckled against Koda's hand, where he still held it against his lips. "Is that a yes?"

A small part of Koda was scared to embrace the happiness. The problem was, he wanted it too badly. "Yes. I would love to stay the night with you."

"Actually, I meant longer than a night."

. . .

"Oh, really?" Koda hadn't meant the question to sound quite so hopeful, but it was too late. He had hoped to sound coy, but his happiness betrayed him.

Felix dropped their linked hands to his lap, but his grip didn't loosen. "I thought I made my intentions clear. We're together. I plan to keep you."

Koda bit his bottom lip, trying hard not to smile like an idiot. He hadn't expected this level of happiness. For now, he planned to cling to it.

The moment he was home, Koda ditched his cane. He nearly sighed in relief to be free of the extra burden. As much as he loved being on vacation, there was no place like home. "If you don't care, I'd love to take a shower before we go."

Felix's fingertips slipped down his arm. "Go for it. I can wait."

. . .

Koda stole a quick kiss before grabbing his bag and heading down the hall. He could feel Felix trailing behind. A small smile touched his lips. If Felix wanted to watch, Koda would give him a show. Koda took his time. First, he peeled off his shirt and tossed it in the laundry basket for his cleaning person. Next, he dumped the rest of his clothes from their trip into the basket as well. Since they had stayed much longer than expected, they had gone shopping for new clothes. His poor overnight bag had barely closed. Koda went to work on packing it with a more reasonable amount of clothing. He moved around the room, feeling of each article of clothing and picking his outfits carefully. As he grabbed a couple of pairs of underwear, his hand brushed the condoms and lube he kept stashed there. His curiosity got the best of him.

"Is it okay if I ask you something?"

"How in the hell did you know I'm here?"

. . .

A smile snapped to Koda's lips at the shock in Felix's voice. "I can feel you looking at me."

A sexy chuckle floated through the air, making goosebumps rise on Koda's skin. "I can't help myself. Your beauty makes me a voyeur. What did you want to ask me?"

Koda fought a strange urge to blush. He didn't lack in confidence. Koda just wasn't used to having compliments so readily heaped upon him. "Is there a reason we didn't have sex this past week?" The question burst from Koda in his rush to hide his embarrassment.

Felix made a slight humming noise, as if thinking over Koda's question. "Honestly, I didn't plan to seduce you. I wanted to get to know you better. Plus, I wanted you to see that I want more from you than sex, so I didn't take any condoms with me." Felix's voice filled with laughter at his confession. "It was kind of like I tried forcing myself to behave by not being prepared. Of course, it didn't exactly happen that way."

That was sweet and hot. Koda didn't want him to behave. "I have condoms." Silence met his announcement, but the air churned with lust. Still, the fact that Felix didn't speak had Koda regretting his impulsive statement. "I should—"

Felix's mouth covered his, making Koda jump. For once, he hadn't felt Felix crossing the room. One second, he had been on one side of the room, and the next, Koda was in Felix's arms. Felix's hands were everywhere. Koda didn't know where to put his. In the end, he forgot he had arms. Felix had a kiss that was mesmerizing. He forced Koda to give it all his attention. Koda didn't know if he would bite, suck, or lick next. It was sexy as hell and made the world disappear.

"Where are these condoms?"

. . .

Koda motioned toward the drawer. He heard Felix rummaging around, and then he was back. His tongue invaded Koda's mouth. He pulled back just as quickly. "This isn't the only reason I'm here."

A smile snapped to Koda's lips. He had never met anyone who worried even a tenth about his feelings as much as Felix did. "I know."

"Good." That was the only warning for Koda before he found himself face down on the mattress with his pants gone.

Breaths stuttered from his lungs as Koda tried regaining his balance. A wrapper crinkled behind him. Koda's muscles tensed. Then the air changed again. Soft lips brushed his spine. Koda's eyes fell closed. His lips parted on a pant. Wet fingers probed his asshole, stretching and massaging. Koda moved restlessly against the mattress. Felix kissed Koda's back while he explored Koda's ass. He didn't play games. Felix found that internal spot that had Koda moaning, and he didn't let up. He rubbed until Koda begged. Then a much bigger appendage took over the job. Koda thought he would go insane.

"Goddamn, baby. Yes. Let me hear how much you like it."

Koda understood Felix's demand, but he was too far gone to think straight. He humped the bed while getting fucked. His head was a mess. Koda should have known Felix would be as big of a perfectionist in the bedroom as he was in the studio. Felix paid attention to the details. His every touch was methodical and perfect. Koda felt special. It was as if Felix thought of nothing except Koda's pleasure. It was erotic and addictive. Koda knew he would compare everyone to Felix now. All he could do was moan and take it. Felix had him fucked up. He felt too much.

Felix's lips brushed the shell of Koda's ear. "I could do this for the rest of my life."

. . .

Koda's heart stopped. Realization struck. He could too. Koda could be happy with Felix. This wasn't temporary. They were in a full-blown relationship and Koda didn't want out. He wanted more. Felix slammed inside him at the perfect angle and a cry tore from Koda's throat. His thoughts scattered. The way his body tensed in anticipation was all that mattered. Koda held his breath, focusing solely on the pleasure. A wave of ecstasy rocked his soul. His cock twitched as cum coated the bed beneath him. Felix cried out against his back. He almost sounded pained. Pride filled Koda's chest. Then his walls started rebuilding. It was out of Koda's control. He had to protect his heart.

Felix kissed his ear. His gasped breaths caressed Koda's skin. "No one will believe you're mine. I'm not worthy."

Koda's heart melted. He couldn't let Felix feel that way. Koda had never been happier. He couldn't destroy the person who made him feel this good. Felix would see. Koda would make him proud. He wouldn't run.

To say that Felix walked around on cloud nine would be the understatement of the year. After sharing a shower, they had finally made it out of the house. Koda had known exactly where he wanted to eat, which had checked another box for Felix. They had eaten, talked, and held hands. People had taken their picture on the sly. It was nice. Felix felt... whole. Life hadn't been like this for him in a long time. He couldn't take his eyes off Koda.

"Let me give you the tour," Felix said as they came through the back door and into his mudroom. He took Koda's bag from him so he could hold Koda's hand. "You're inside my mudroom. You can leave your shoes here."

"Okay." Koda toed off his shoes and pushed them out of the way with his foot. "What's next?"

"We're headed into the kitchen." Felix paused as they stepped inside the kitchen. "You know, it's just occurred to me you might not need much of a tour. My house is set up pretty similar to your mom's place. My furniture is set up a bit different in the living room and I come in through the back door instead of the front, but it's pretty close. The pool is even in the same spot."

Koda flashed him a gorgeous smile. "That's good to know. I should be able to find the bathroom."

Felix shook his head. He couldn't stop smiling. "Come on. I'll take you to my room and drop off your bag."

"Lead the way."

Hand in hand, Felix led Koda down the hall. A majority of the downstairs was taken up by the entertainment area. Kitchen, dining room, living room, den, and his office. There was only one bedroom on the main floor. It was huge, and it was his. Felix led Koda inside. "This is my room." He looked around, ensuring nothing littered the floor and hindered Koda.

Koda let go of Felix's hand and made his way around the room. Between his cane and feeling of each piece of furniture, Koda seemed to be fine. He stopped at the open bathroom door and motioned in its direction. "Bathroom?"

Felix bit back a chuckle. "Yep."

Koda's smile was everything. "I told you I would find it. This place is set up like my mom's. Her bedroom is the same. Let me guess. Vanity and toilet on the right. Walk-in shower and tub on the left."

"You're partially right." Felix crossed the room and came to stand at Koda's side. "I had the bathroom remodeled, so now the left side of the room is a wet room. You head through a set of glass doors and there's a claw-foot tub on the right and showerheads to the left." A thought occurred to him Felix had never thought to ask Koda before now. "Do you know how to read Braille?"

"I do."

At Koda's enthusiastic response, Felix touched the small of his back and urged him inside the bathroom. "Awesome. Come check this out." He led Koda to the control panel outside the wet room. Felix took Koda's hand and showed him the buttons. "This is the control panel, and the door is to the left of it."

Koda felt of the buttons. Each one had tiny bumps for the blind. Felix had never thought much about it until now. His gaze slid Koda's way. A lump formed in his throat. It was almost like he was shown a tiny sign. Koda was meant to be here. Koda's face turned Felix's way. A sexy smile stretched his lips. "You might have to drag me out of here in the morning. This thing has everything."

"Or I could join you in the morning."

.   .   .

Koda's smile turned wicked. "Or you could join me."

For a long moment, they stood in silence. Felix stared at Koda while hope grew in his chest. They really were going places. He felt giddy as hell and a little nervous. Felix was fucking happy as could be, and he was a tad bit scared. He didn't want to lose Koda. Right now, he wanted to sit and listen to Koda talk for the rest of the night.

"Would you like some coffee?"

Before Koda could answer, his phone butted in. "Incoming text from Cade. Cade: Are you fucking kidding me? Please tell me the tabloids are lying and you're not dating Felix."

Felix winced. Before he could say a word, another text rolled in right behind Cade's.

.   .   .

"Incoming text from Zayn. Zayn: You're just friends, huh? I don't appreciate you making me look like a fool."

Koda released a grunted laugh.

Felix couldn't see the humor. "No one will congratulate you for dating me."

Koda dug out his phone. "I don't need anyone's praise. I'm proud of myself for snagging you." He pressed a button on the side of his phone. "Send a reply to Cade and Zayn. Mind your fucking business." A smile snapped to Felix's lips as Koda shoved his phone back in his pocket. "You were saying about that coffee..."

Felix couldn't stop staring at Koda and smiling. "What did I do to deserve you?"

. . .

Koda's expression turned heated. He snagged the collar of Felix's shirt and lured him closer. "You shoved your way past my bullshit and refused to budge. Plus, I know you. You deserve the moon." He pressed a sweet kiss to Felix's lips and Felix was lost. He knew there was no coming back from this moment. There would be no coffee or conversations tonight. He felt too much. Felix needed to hold Koda. Kiss him. Nothing mattered beyond that.

SIX

FELIX: *Can I see you tonight?*

Koda: *I would be pissed if you didn't.*

Felix: *Good. It's a date.*

Koda: *Dinner at my place?*

Felix: *I'll be there.*

Felix: *I was thinking, since we're always together anyhow, and sometimes you're stuck waiting for me to get off work, how would you feel about me giving you a key?*

Koda: *I think it would make it easier for me to be waiting nude in your bed tonight.*

Felix: *I left it under the flowerpot on the front porch.*

Felix: *I can't wait to be inside you.*

Koda: *My entire dry-cleaning place just heard you say that.*

Felix: *Good. They'll know to get ready for more ruined clothes.*

The usual chatter of his overly loud family surrounded Koda. He listened to the conversations buzzing around him, but he really only cared to hear one voice. Occasionally, he heard Felix's faint "excuse me" as he worked to grab Koda a second plate of food. It tickled Koda that even after five months of dating and countless visits with his family, Felix still hadn't learned to simply elbow his way in and fuck everyone's feelings. He supposed Felix's way worked. Everyone loved him. In fact, Koda's family and friends were always more excited to see Felix than they were him. Even Zayn had been won over by Felix's charm. Koda had been too, if he was being honest. He couldn't get enough. Every second together wasn't enough time to appease Koda's greedy heart.

"So... when are you two getting married and adopting me some grandbabies?" Elena asked as she filled Felix's empty seat next to Koda.

· · ·

Koda covered his face with both hands. His mom was impossible. "You did not just ask me that."

She had zero shame. "What? You two are so happy together and that's the natural course of things. You meet, fall in love, get married, and raise kids. The circle of life."

He loved his mom. Koda had to remind himself of that sometimes. He took a breath and tried being rational. "I recognize that's the way things usually go, but you're presuming a lot. First, we haven't been dating that long. Felix doesn't love me, and it's only been like a year or so since he went through an ugly divorce. He does not want to marry me. Don't rush this."

Elena blew out a raspberry. "Please. Spare me. I just watched that man swipe the last of the fruit salad from beneath your aunt's nose. You know damn well that fruit salad is for you and your aunt Gabby is mean as shit and crazy enough to stab someone over her favorite foods. That's love, baby."

. . .

The only reason Koda kept smiling was because he was happy as hell with Felix. Everything else at the current moment was a nightmare. He knew his mom. She had this idea in her head now. Every time he saw her from now on, she would harp about this. He also knew Felix. Felix wasn't in love, or he would have said it. Not to mention, Felix's divorce had been epically nasty. Koda didn't imagine Felix would ever want to marry again. Koda couldn't get that in his head, only to end up disappointed. He only just learned to feel safe in a long-term relationship. Koda couldn't let himself dream too big.

"I snagged the last of the fruit salad for you," Felix said, pushing a plate into Koda's hands. Koda felt his mom practically melt away, leaving them alone. Felix reclaimed his seat at Koda's side. "I had to nab it before Gabby, and she smacked my ass for stealing it. You're worth it." Koda could hear the smile in Felix's voice. The sound had him beaming.

. . .

"I appreciate your sacrifice. No one makes fruit salad like Mom. It's the coconut." Koda scooped a bite into his mouth and savored Felix's thievery on his behalf.

"It's your turn, Felix."

At the yelled words, Felix was back on his feet. "Sorry, baby. I'll be back in a few. It seems I'm up for horseshoes."

Koda flashed a smile. It slipped away as longing hit when Felix's lips touched the corner of Koda's mouth. Koda wanted to turn his head and take the kiss he craved. He was much happier than anyone knew. Felix had taken over Koda's every thought in the past several months. He was lost. Fuck, he wished his mom hadn't used the big "M" word. Koda had never wanted anyone the way he needed Felix. They were perfect together.

"I must say, I love your man."

. . .

Koda hurriedly ate his fruit salad as Gabby stole Felix's chair. She was always mean, but she had been extra cruel to Koda his whole life. He didn't doubt for a second she would swipe the food right from his mouth if he wasn't fast enough. "He's awesome," Koda said around his food.

"Don't know what he sees in you, though."

Koda swallowed and tried to stay calm at her jibe. Everyone had at least one Gabby in their family. She was old, evil, and loved to drive a stake in Koda's heart every time they spoke. Usually, she liked to joke about his physique—like he should work out more but also gain weight. The last time she cornered him, she claimed he was balding. He always tried avoiding her. It seemed he wouldn't be so lucky today.

"I wouldn't know, since I can't see," Koda mumbled, hoping she would go away.

. . .

Gabby smacked his knee. "That's a good point. You took the words right out of my mouth. He's a really nice man. Maybe he's doing his Christian duty by dating someone less fortunate." Gabby released a loud and wheezing bark of laughter at her words, as if she impressed herself with that insult. "Mark my words, though. You'll never get that one to fall in love with you, much less drag him to the altar. If I were you, I'd get all the pity fucks I can before he disappears."

"I forgot to bring you a drink."

Koda startled at the sudden appearance of Felix at his side. His empty plate disappeared, and a cold drink found its way into his hand. Before Koda could thank Felix, Felix's lips touched his in a very passionate and public kiss. Everything else melted away. He forgot to let Gabby's words hurt.

Felix pulled away just enough to press his forehead to Koda's. "I love you."

. . .

"I love you too." The admission slipped easily from Koda's lips before he truly realized what happened.

Felix shifted positions as if going down onto his knees beside Koda's chair. "I've been meaning to talk to you about something important, but it seems like there's never a right time."

Koda was so focused on Felix that it took him a second to realize the entire backyard had fallen silent. There was no music. No kids screamed in the background. All chatter had died. It was as if the entire party held a collective breath.

A nervous chuckle escaped Koda. "Did I miss something? Why do I feel like everyone is staring at us?"

"Because they are." The heavy humor in Felix's voice didn't ease the growing tension inside Koda. "I didn't plan to do this today, so I don't have a ring with me."

. . .

"What?" Even to Koda's ears, he sounded as lost as he felt.

An evil-sounding chuckle fell from Felix's lips and caressed Koda's skin. "Will you marry me, Koda?"

Koda floundered. He didn't know what to say. Then it hit him. Felix had overheard Gabby's hateful words. He was rescuing Koda, and Koda was making him wait. "Yes." The unsurety was there for anyone listening. Koda couldn't help it. The entire situation felt like a cosmic joke. He finally fell in love and the man he wanted was forced to stage a mock declaration of love and marriage proposal to save him from a spiteful family member. People cheered like it was real. Felix kissed him like he meant it. Koda's heart broke. He needed a drink.

"I'll break open the good liquor, so we can toast."

. . .

At Elena's words, Koda nearly sighed in relief. Thank fuck. He was about to get shit-faced. There was no other way to handle this day. Koda had never hated anything more than he despised having this moment stolen from him. Maybe one day life would be fair. Today wasn't that day.

Felix was furious. More than that. He was enraged. Gabby's hateful words burrowed beneath his skin and ate away at his brain. Koda's expression had been the worst part. He looked crushed. Things hadn't improved because now Koda was plastered— like a man who had a romantic declaration of love and proposal stolen from him. There was no fixing it. Felix had never been angrier in his life. That was saying a lot.

Koda leaned heavily on Felix as they came through Felix's back door all the way to their bed. "I'm sorry."

Felix's heart turned over in his chest at Koda's muttered words as he helped Koda undress. "Why are you apologizing? You're allowed to cut loose just like anyone else. I'll always be here to take care of you afterward."

In an exaggerated motion, Koda shook his head. "I'm sorry you had to pretend to love me and fake a marriage proposal. All because my aunt is the devil."

Felix froze. It hadn't occurred to him that Koda would think Felix hadn't meant every word he said today. Koda looked defeated, sitting on the edge of Felix's bed with no shirt and his shoulders sagging. Felix crowded Koda's space. He kept moving until he had Koda on his back and covered Koda's body.

With his weight braced on his arms, Felix brushed his nose against Koda's. "Are you saying you don't love me?"

He felt Koda go still. "No. I'm not saying that."

. . .

Felix placed a soft kiss at the corner of Koda's mouth. "Then tell me."

"I love you."

The sweet way Koda said the words had the backs of Felix's eyes burning. "I love you too." He nuzzled Koda's nose again. "Are you saying you don't want to marry me?"

Felix heard Koda's breath catch. "I'm not saying that either."

Felix lured Koda into a kiss. "Then tell me," Felix said, cajoling Koda between kisses. "I want to hear that you want me the way I want you."

"I want to marry you."

. . .

Their lips met and lingered. Felix's chest warmed. There had been no act. Gabby might have forced Felix's hand, but this was real. Felix wouldn't go down on one knee for just anyone, and he would not let Koda feel cheated. A thought occurred to him. Maybe there was a small way he could improve the situation. "I do have a ring, but I wanted to ask you about it first."

Koda cupped Felix's face, as if trying to make him be still as he held Felix's attention. "You have a ring."

Felix nodded. "It belonged to my grandfather. I wanted to make sure you were okay with that. If you would rather I buy you something else, I understand."

"You want to give me your grandfather's ring."

Felix didn't know why Koda kept repeating everything Felix said. "If you want it?"

. . .

"I want it."

After another quick kiss, Felix rolled away and headed for the closet. He pushed some clothes aside and opened the safe built into the wall. It took a second of searching before he found the velvet box that came to him when his grandfather passed. While it was true Felix had made a great living by himself, he also came from money. His grandfather had been a popular stage actor, and he had left everything he owned to Felix's mother and him to be split between them. But he had been adamant Felix get his ring.

Felix popped open the box. It was a dome eternity ring with diamonds set all the way around the rose-gold piece. His grandfather's attorney had valued the piece at around ten thousand dollars. It was worth way more than that to Felix. He had been the only grandchild and his grandfather had been his best friend. Even though they had only been dating five months, there was no one else Felix could imagine wearing this ring.

· · ·

With ring in hand, Felix headed back to bed. He crawled onto the mattress and straddled Koda's waiting body. Koda looked serene—like peace had been restored inside him since learning Felix meant his proposal.

"Would you like to inspect it before I put it on?"

Koda shook his head. "I've had a lot to drink. Maybe it's best you put it on first."

Felix took Koda's left hand between his hands and slipped the ring on his finger. To Felix's shock, it fit like it was meant to be there. It was like a sign, because the ring couldn't be resized. Felix had thought to wear it himself when he first inherited the piece, but it was too small for him. A jeweler had explained, because of the diamonds, it couldn't be expanded. Now Felix realized it had been waiting on a different home. Felix kissed Koda's hand before releasing it.

. . .

Koda felt of the piece, tracing the diamonds. "Holy shit. I love it. It fits perfectly."

"I love you and I think Grandpa approves of my choice."

Koda's eyes filled with tears. "It's not fair that you were coerced into asking me to marry you. If you want to take it back..."

Felix covered Koda's mouth with his before Koda found the words to finish that sentence. Maybe he had proposed way earlier than he intended. Felix had no regrets. Koda had said yes, and—honestly—Felix had fully expected it would take years for Koda to be ready for marriage. After all, they had gone into this relationship with the looming idea Koda would panic and run. Instead, they had been inseparable and now they would be married. Felix wasn't scared. His ugly divorce hadn't broken him. Felix liked being a husband. Now he would be Koda's. Wow. He couldn't wait.

. . .

Their kiss turned passionate as Felix's jeans loosened at the waist. "Fuck. I really do love you. I need you to know that," Felix said as he kissed his way to Koda's neck.

"I feel it."

At Koda's claim, the day hit Felix like a truck. Koda had admitted to loving him. That in itself was a miracle. Then Koda had agreed to marry him. Felix didn't understand how he had gotten so lucky. He needed Koda to feel just as blessed. Felix kissed a path down Koda's body while working on getting Koda out of his pants. Koda stopped him.

"Wait."

Felix froze. He wasn't one to suck dick and likely he wasn't very good at it, but he loved Koda. They would be together forever. He would get better at it. "If you don't want me to—"

. . .

"I'm going to be sick."

It hit Felix that the alcohol had finally caught up to Koda. He had Koda on his feet and draped over the toilet in no time. A ridiculous smile stretched Felix's lips as he rubbed Koda's back while Koda heaved. He had never been happier to be in this position because he was with Koda.

Koda gasped for air with his face hovering over the throne. "I'm sorry for ruining our night."

Felix blew out a raspberry as he settled down next to Koda on the floor. "Don't be ridiculous. I'm with you. There's no place else I'd rather be."

Koda's chuckle echoed through the bathroom. "I love you. I promise I won't drink on our wedding day."

"Yeah. You definitely can't handle it."

. . .

Their laughter filled the bathroom, and Felix realized it would always be this way. Koda and him against the world. The first time Koda had been in this bathroom, he had chosen Felix over his friends. Now here they were celebrating their engagement. Felix couldn't ask for more. He was marrying his best friend.

SEVEN

DESPITE FELIX'S constant fears of having rushed Koda, Koda married him without a single hint of doubt. Throughout planning their wedding, Felix held his breath, expecting Koda to call things off any second. Koda never let him down. He jumped right in with Felix and Elena to plan a gorgeous wedding and reception. Until the moment Koda said his vows, Felix still expected to lose everything. Koda never let that happen. Now Felix couldn't take his eyes off his husband. A smile tugged at his lips as he watched Elena drag Koda from person to person at their reception, ensuring everyone knew her son had married, as if they didn't know why they were there. Felix loved everything about them. He never expected his life to be this good.

. . .

"You chose well."

Felix bit back a smile at his mom's cold-sounding remark—like it physically drained her to say something nice. She wasn't known for her loving nature. "Thank you. I'm surprised you noticed since this is only the second time you've met him... at our wedding, no less."

Priscilla turned her head and eyed him as if he had lost his mind. "I only needed to meet Megan once to know I didn't like her. Since I was right, I don't see your point."

"I guess I don't have one." Felix was just glad she had shown up. He loved his mom, but she wasn't like Koda's mom. Elena had fussed over Koda all day, making sure his tux was perfect, his hair was flawless, and continuously hugging him. Felix didn't come from that family. His mom loved him in her own way. Felix was self-aware enough to recognize that was why he fell in love so easily. He had spent his entire life looking for someone to love him back. Even after years of marriage to Megan, he had never felt loved unconditionally. For the first time in his life, Felix was certain he had found that.

Priscilla set her hand on his knee. "I don't think this one cares anything about your money. That's a rare find."

Felix tore his gaze away from Koda again to stare at his mom. She looked nothing like him. He had brown hair. Her once blonde hair was now white. His light blue eyes matched his grandfather's. Priscilla had gotten her mother's green eyes. There was nothing of Priscilla in Felix's features. Sometimes, he wished he could find a common ground with her.

"He has his own money."

. . .

Priscilla nodded. "That's good. A marriage built on love is always best."

Felix would take her praise at face value. Honestly, he had expected her to say something about Koda being blind. She hadn't. That impressed him. She probably knew the truth as much as anyone. The only blind person in their relationship was Felix. Koda had been right beneath his nose for years, and Felix hadn't seen him. So much heartbreak could have been avoided in his life if only he had paid attention. The love of his life had been right there all along.

Zayn materialized while Felix was lost in thought. He held his hand out and Felix automatically shook it. "Congrats, man."

A bright smile snapped to Felix's lips. No matter who congratulated him, Felix would never tire of being proud. "Thank you."

. . .

Zayn filled the empty seat meant for Koda. "Yeah, I really expected to be jealous today, but nope. You two are meant to be. Anyone can see it when they look at you."

"I appreciate it." Felix didn't know how else to respond. While Zayn had been a pretty good sport about Koda choosing Felix, Felix had still kept one eye on him anytime he was nearby. He always expected Zayn to pull Koda aside and try to undermine their relationship. It never happened.

Koda returned to his side. Felix snagged Koda's waist and pulled him into his lap before Koda accidentally sat in Zayn's, since Zayn had stolen his seat. Koda didn't complain. "Hey, gorgeous. I think Mom has finally finished making me greet the thousand family members she invited."

Before Felix could respond, Priscilla shocked him speechless by taking one of Koda's hands. "You're a good boy. I'm sure your mother just wants everyone to see it for themselves."

Koda's muscles relaxed in Felix's arms. "Awww. Thank you."

Felix opened his mouth to suggest they head upstairs to their honeymoon suite. Zayn cut him off. "Who is this DJ? He's amazing."

Felix's gaze automatically slid toward the tables where Spencer stood behind his laptops and speakers. Headphones covered his ears, and he moved to the beat of the music. "That's Zealous Blaze."

Zayn did a double take. "*The* Zealous Blaze?"

Zayn's reaction didn't surprise Felix. Zealous was the number one DJ in the world. Everyone knew his name, but not everyone recognized his face, since most of the people who partied at his raves never got close enough to him to see him.

. . .

Koda jumped in to explain on Felix's behalf. "His real name is Spencer. He's been friends with Felix for years. They met back when Felix first started his production label. He never does weddings, but he insisted on doing this one. You'd love him."

The way Zayn's gaze didn't budge from Spencer had Felix ready to agree. Zayn already looked like he loved him. Priscilla cut in before Felix could suggest that Zayn go introduce himself.

"You should head upstairs now so people can blow their bubbles at you. I guarantee most people are waiting for you two to leave before they go."

"I agree with this decision," Koda said, jumping to his feet.

Hunger roared to life at Koda's enthusiasm. It seemed Felix wasn't alone in his desire to get their honeymoon started. Felix had been dying to get inside Koda since the moment he had kissed the groom. There was something about knowing they were married. Felix's possessiveness had tripled in size. He wanted to be alone with Koda. Felix needed to hear Koda say he was happy... that he had no regrets. He knew it was crazy. Felix couldn't help it. There wasn't a single thing Felix had done in his life to deserve Koda. He kept waiting to have the rug ripped out from beneath him. The way it always was when he was too happy.

Felix stood and took Koda's hand. The music stopped and Spencer's voice filled the air. "The grooms have decided to depart. Everyone give them the sendoff they deserve."

Applause filled the air as everyone scrambled to follow them from the hotel ballroom all the way to the elevator, blowing bubbles around them.

Koda laughed as the elevator doors closed, finally giving them a second alone. "I feel like I just got slapped by a million tiny dish soap kisses."

. . .

Felix's face hurt from smiling. He invaded Koda's space. "How about a real kiss to make things better?"

Koda's tone changed, turning sultry. "I like this plan." His hands slid up Felix's chest before locking behind Felix's neck. Felix's body stirred as he lowered his head and claimed Koda's lips. They wouldn't be on the elevator forever, but Felix planned to set the mood now. This was the first night of the rest of their lives. It would be happy and filled with love. Just like their marriage would be. Felix intended to see to that. Koda was his whole heart. Felix would cherish him as such.

If Koda ever stopped to look at things too closely, it was odd to know that a mere seven months ago, life had been completely different. Koda had been certain that Felix was a fling, and Koda expected to run at the first hint of permanency. Then he hadn't. Koda could point at that singular moment and say it was the deciding factor of his entire future. He hadn't run. Koda had chosen happiness. He thanked God for that every day.

. . .

Koda became completely dependent upon Felix getting him safely to their room. He stayed focused on kissing Felix and trying to divest his new husband of his clothing. Thankfully, they had an entire floor to themselves. Their room key took them to the penthouse and the elevator doors opened into their room. Even though Koda had no plans to leave here until it was time for their flight to Maui, he appreciated Felix describing their surroundings to him earlier in the day. That was just one of the many ways Felix was perfect. The moment the elevator dinged and Koda heard the doors slide open, he went straight for the button on Felix's pants. He had no shame. Koda wanted to savor his new title of husband. Damn, it had a good ring. Koda never expected to have this life. Yet here he was. Koda needed to be as close as possible to Felix now. He couldn't wait.

"I love you. Don't make me wait." Koda didn't care if he sounded desperate. He was.

. . .

"I've got you."

Felix kept his word. Koda's clothes disappeared in a fast series of pulls and tugs. Felix kissed and bit while steering Koda toward what Koda hoped would be the nearest flat surface. A moan escaped him when his back touched the mattress. By the time Felix's nude body met his and wet fingers stretched his asshole, Koda was ready to scream. He felt crazed with need.

"Please?" As the plea left his lips, Felix's dick shoved inside him. Koda clung to Felix's shoulders and took everything Felix dished out. Felix's teeth scraped Koda's chest while he sawed in and out of Koda's ass. Koda threw his arm up and his hand collided with the headboard. He braced himself and fought to get closer. It was violent until the first spasm hit.

As he gasped for air through the waves of pleasure, Felix settled into a slower pace. His kisses turned sweet. Koda's eyes stung. Before Felix, Koda hadn't known this much happiness existed in the world. He definitely hadn't known it could be his.

"I love you," Felix gasped as his body jerked in Koda's arms.

Koda buried his short fingernails into Felix's skin, trying desperately to get a hair closer to him. He would never be close enough to satisfy his heart.

"I love you." Koda cupped Felix's face and held on. "I can't believe you're mine."

Their foreheads touched, and they didn't move. Koda could feel the love rolling off Felix in waves. He savored every moment while praying this feeling would grow even stronger until they were unbreakable. Koda never wanted to be anywhere else. He had found his home in Felix's arms. Koda had never been so scared of losing something.

· · ·

For what felt like hours, Koda snuggled with Felix without saying a word. Truthfully, there was a small part of him that was in shock. Since the day Koda first invited Felix to his parents' house, he had been completely caught up in a whirlwind. Now that they were married, Koda felt like he took his first calming breath in ages. He was struck anew by everything they had been through.

"I think this is what people mean when they talk about how they just know."

Felix's arms tightened around Koda. "I was just thinking the same thing. It seems like I should feel overwhelmed, but I don't. I just feel like everything is how it should be. I'm here, married to my best friend and the love of my life—like it's just that simple."

"Like it's too easy," Koda said, adding to Felix's thoughts.

. . .

"Exactly. Everyone always says that anything worth having is worth fighting for, so you automatically feel like nothing good comes easy. Now I'm seeing how wrong that thought pattern has been my entire life. If I had just accepted things shouldn't be so hard, I wouldn't have been so blindly determined to hang on to things that weren't meant for me. I would've looked for you sooner. In a way, I'm resentful of all the years I spent without holding you like this."

Koda took a deep breath, inhaling the scent of Felix's cologne. He felt more at home than he ever had in his life. "I think it's safe to say that life has definitely been waiting for us to finally realize we were each other's soul mate all along."

"Damn." Felix's happy-sounding curse made Koda smile. That one word summed everything up perfectly. Maybe they had come together at exactly the moment they were meant to fall, or maybe they had both been completely oblivious, missing out on years of happiness. Koda supposed they would never know. Damn.

EIGHT

SINCE MARRYING Koda three months ago, Felix still hadn't stopped floating on air. They spent every second together and neither of them tired of it. Felix didn't doubt for a second, if he lived to be one hundred and could do this for the next sixty years, he still wouldn't tire of being with Koda. Shit, he couldn't even walk away from the booth's window and stop watching Koda while he worked.

There was something about watching Koda lose himself to the beat. He was here, but he wasn't. A part of Koda disappeared inside the songs he sang, making each new track perfect. He was the icing on every album he graced. While Koda immersed himself in the music, Felix lost himself watching Koda work. He was magic, and Felix was the luckiest man on earth.

"You have a visitor."

At Mike's announcement, Felix tore his gaze away from Koda and glanced toward the front. Megan stood waiting. Felix's heart skipped a beat as dread washed over him. His feet refused to budge, and his throat wouldn't work. He hadn't seen her since the judge signed their divorce papers. Felix didn't care to see her now, yet he couldn't look away. She was pregnant.

When Felix made no move to greet her, Megan crossed the room. The closer she came, the angrier Felix got. She had no right to be here. They were over. If she wanted to rub it in his face that she had finally achieved what he couldn't, then she had chosen the wrong man. Felix wanted nothing else to do with her. Time had not healed his anger.

·　·　·

"I'm married," Felix said the moment she was within earshot.

A slight smile touched her lips. "I know."

Felix's face screwed up in a combination of anger and confusion. "Then why are you here? I know you're not about to claim that baby is mine to get child support."

Megan took an audible breath, and it hit Felix that she didn't look so good. "I know you're understandably angry with me, Felix, but could we just not."

She sounded tired and there were dark circles under her eyes. Her red hair looked lifeless, and she seemed thinner despite her rounded belly. Felix's anger melted away. "Yeah. Okay. What do you need?"

. . .

Megan's gaze slid toward the booth where Koda worked. "Is it okay if I talk to you and Koda in private?"

Felix glanced around and motioned for Mike. "Hey, Mike. Could you grab Koda from the booth and ask him to join us in my office?"

With a nod, Mike jumped to do as Felix asked. Felix led Megan inside his office. Before he could offer Megan a seat, Koda appeared in the doorway.

Megan smiled at the sight of him. "Hey, Koda. You look good."

A bright smile lit Koda's face, surprising Felix. "Long time no see, Meg. Where's my hug?"

Megan hugged Koda. She didn't let go. Neither did Koda. Megan's eyes filled with tears, but she didn't make a sound. Koda went still, as if he could feel her pain. He rubbed her back.

"Tell me what's wrong."

Felix's throat swelled as he watched the exchange, but his chest filled with pride. He had married such a good man. Felix didn't know what he had done to deserve him. Seeing Megan again took him straight back to feeling like the biggest piece of shit on the planet.

Megan pulled away and swiped at her eyes. "Do you mind if I sit down? I'm not feeling so great."

Felix moved to offer her a chair before shutting his office door. Koda pulled a chair close to Megan's side and reached for her hand. Megan looked like she might fall apart at any moment, but she held tight to Koda, as if drawing strength from him.

. . .

The moment Felix's ass hit the chair behind his desk, Megan dropped the bomb. "I have cancer."

Koda sat back hard, as if his spine gave out.

Felix opened his mouth to say he didn't know what, but Megan cut him off.

"It's aggressive, and that means so too is the treatment. There's only one problem." Megan ran her hand over rounded belly.

"You're pregnant."

At Felix's unnecessary pointing out of the obvious, Koda's head turned Megan's way. "You're pregnant?"

Megan nodded as if Koda could see. "Five months along. It's a boy."

. . .

"Oh, Megan." Koda sounded every bit as heartbroken as he should. Felix had told Koda the stories of how hard they had fought to get pregnant and the toll it had taken on them when they couldn't. A baby would be everything to Megan.

Megan took a ragged-sounding breath before barreling ahead. "My baby would not survive killing the cancer and they say I likely won't live longer than six months without treatment." Megan rubbed her stomach, as if caressing her child. Her gaze never wavered from Felix. "You know what I went through and what it cost me to conceive. After our divorce, I took a long look at myself and I knew that I didn't want another man. All I wanted was to be a mom. That's it. I don't have any family other than my sister, and she lives twenty-two hundred miles away. This baby was supposed to be my family. I was starting a whole new chapter. Now..." Megan shrugged, looking crushed and lost.

"What do you need us to do?" Koda asked, taking over while Felix had no words. This had been his wife. Maybe they had ended badly and hated each other, but they had loved each other first. That was all that mattered now.

Megan visibly swallowed as her gaze moved between them. She looked scared as hell. "I can't let this baby die. Even at the cost of my life, I can't do it. Maybe I'm crazy and I'm sure a lot of people would make a different choice, but I can't. I love this baby too much."

Koda nodded as he patted Megan's hand. "You have to be the one to make that decision."

"I want you two to raise my baby."

Felix's gaze shot to Koda.

Koda had gone completely still.

. . .

Megan didn't give them time to recover from their shock. "Like I said, Rachel lives twenty-two hundred miles away, and she already has five kids. Her husband is unemployed, and I can't ask this of her."

"But you can ask it of me?" The question was out there before Felix could think straight. He couldn't help what his mouth said in his shock.

To his surprise, Megan smiled. "You're perfect for the job. I know you don't owe me anything, but I guess I always thought we would be parents together someday. You're the only person I can trust to give my baby the best life. I know you would make sure he knows me, even though I won't be there. There isn't a single doubt in my mind you would love him like a stranger never could."

Felix floundered. "This is asking a lot."

"I know it is," Megan shot back just as quickly.

. . .

"Can we think about it?" Koda asked, saving Felix from himself. He still looked as if Megan had slapped him, but Koda was at least calmer than Felix.

Megan's shoulders relaxed as she looked Koda's way. "Of course. I don't expect an answer today. I just don't have much time left to get things settled." Megan stood. "I'll look for your call. Thank you for listening."

Felix stood, even though he didn't know why. Megan gave him a small wave as she slipped out the door, leaving the mess from her bomb behind. Felix dropped back into his chair. He stared at Koda, willing him to say something. Koda sat in complete silence, as if his mind had gone away.

Felix couldn't take anymore. "Say something."

Koda's face turned his way. "What do you want me to say?"

· · ·

Felix wanted Koda to scream and throw things, because that was what he wanted to do. "Say you don't want this baby and I'll tell her no."

"I can't say that."

Koda's calm acceptance fed Felix's anger and hurt. Megan was dying and there was nothing he could do. She had turned his world upside down—again—and he was helpless against it. "Why can't you say that?"

"Because you want this baby and you'll resent me if I say I don't."

Felix's shoulders fell. He had started the day so happy and carefree. Life never went that way for him. "I want you. You're the person I love and you're the person I'm spending the rest of my life with. Nothing matters more to me than us. I will never resent you if you say this isn't what you want."

. . .

For a long moment, Koda didn't react. He dropped his chin to his chest as if he could no longer hold up the weight of his thoughts. His shoulders expanded as he took a deep breath. Felix thought his mind would snap while he waited for Koda to say the words that would decide their future, because Felix could not make this decision. He just couldn't. Finally, Koda's chin lifted. His expression was way too serene for Felix's liking.

"Maybe you wouldn't resent me, but I would hate myself. We should do the right thing."

Fuck. Koda's choice of words didn't bring on the feeling of resolution. Felix felt like a nail had been hammered in their coffin—like he was watching the first moment of Koda falling out of love with their marriage. He couldn't take it.

"I'll tell her no."

. . .

Koda shook his head. "That's not an option and you know it. Plus, you never know. Lots of people are told they won't live out the year and then they survive. It happened to me. I might be blind now, but otherwise, you'd never know I had a life-altering brain tumor. Megan might have this baby, get her aggressive treatment, and live to tell about it. For now, though, we can offer her some peace of mind. The stress can't be good for her."

The tightness in Felix's chest eased. Koda was right. Lots of people lived after they were told they wouldn't. He was panicking over something that might never happen. Plus, she obviously hadn't told Rachel yet. Rachel likely wouldn't be onboard with Megan giving her child to Felix. No matter her circumstances, Rachel would want that baby.

NINE

MEGAN: *Lawyer's appointment at ten.*

Felix: *Okay.*

Koda: *We'll be there.*

———

Megan: *I have an ultrasound today if you'd like to come and see the baby.*

Felix: *Can't. I'm busy.*

Megan: *My attorney has your copy of the adoption papers ready.*

Felix: *Okay.*

Megan: *How do you feel about going to my next OB appointment with me? Felix isn't interested.*

Koda: *Felix is crazy busy. He picked up a new big-name client who wants to redo their entire backlist.*

Megan: *I know when I'm being avoided. I was married to him for years. You didn't answer my question.*

Koda: *Sorry. Of course, I'll go.*

. . .

Megan: *I'll pick you up tomorrow at eleven.*

Koda: *How about I hire us a car and we can go to lunch afterward? You don't need to be driving.*

Megan: *That sounds great, actually. Thank you.*

Koda: *See you then.*

Despite Koda's fears that Megan's request would hurt his marriage, nothing changed. In fact, it was almost eerie. It was as if Felix worked twice as hard to keep Koda happy for fear of losing him over Megan's baby. As the days drew closer to baby Liam's delivery date, Felix grew quieter and Koda spent every day on edge. They were fine, but it was like this terrible thing hid just out of sight, waiting to ruin them. Koda didn't know how to talk about it, and Felix refused to.

. . .

Megan hadn't been content with a simple yes. Nor had she accepted their legal signatures on documents naming them as Liam's parents upon her death. Megan tried like hell to get them involved in every aspect of her pregnancy. While Felix staunchly refused to take part, Koda found himself sitting in a chair inside Megan's exam room, waiting with her to see the doctor. He still didn't know why he had agreed to this. Mostly, it was because he understood. Koda knew what it was like to stand on the edge of death, knowing there was nothing he could do to change it. It was a lonely place to be.

An unexpected snort broke through their uncomfortable silence. "You know, to this day, I don't understand my thought process at these appointments. I mean, I know they're about to have a whole hand inside me, but I just realized I'm still hiding my panties from sight. Everything about that confession probably makes you grateful you're blind."

A smile pulled at the corners of Koda's mouth. "I doubt anyone would let me stay otherwise."

. . .

A soft knock landed on the door. "How are you today, Megan? I see you have Dad with you today." He felt the man move closer. "I'm Dr. Wells."

Koda held out his hand. A smooth, cool hand clasped his in a quick shake. "Koda."

"Nice to meet you, Koda."

The doctor fell into a litany with Megan while Koda reeled. He never expected to be called Dad. Koda didn't know how to feel. Over the last couple of months, he had tried hard not to feel anything at all about this situation. While he knew there was this real and looming possibility that he would soon be raising someone else's child, Koda didn't know if he wanted this. He loved Felix. That was all he could tell himself each time this reality unexpectedly slapped him in the face. Felix pretended this baby wasn't real. Maybe Koda did a little too. There was a part of him that didn't want to get attached. If

Megan lived, they would never see this child. It was such a strange position for him.

A steady heartbeat filled the air, pulling Koda from his thoughts. "Your boy sounds great today. I still think I should send you across the hall for an ultrasound. You've already dilated a little, but I don't think you'll go into labor any time soon. Your vitals and a few of your test results are a little off, so I would just feel better if we had a look at him."

"Okay. Sounds good."

Paper crackled, and they chatted a bit more. Koda couldn't hear anything but that heartbeat and the exhaustion in Megan's voice. The air felt thinner. This was a real baby. Koda didn't know if he could do this. Sometimes, he didn't do that great of a job of taking care of himself. This would likely be his child. Damn. He felt small in the face of things.

. . .

"I'll let you get dressed and then my nurse will come get you to take you across the hall."

"All right. Thank you."

Koda listened to Megan struggle to stand after the doctor left. He felt like he should say something, but he didn't know where to start. Before he knew it would happen, the truth popped out.

"I'm not sure I know my place anymore."

Megan sounded like she struggled to breathe when she responded. "There's a lot of that going around in this situation. Everything..."

Koda's forehead screwed up in confusion when Megan didn't continue. "Are you okay?"

. . .

Her breathing sounded ragged and something crashed to the floor. "Megan?" Koda stood and felt for her. She was on the floor. Koda's heart stopped before racing into his throat. Koda flew to his feet and called for help. Everything slowed, becoming surreal. He didn't know what was happening or what to do. All Koda knew was he wished Felix was there.

It was a simple, frantic call from Koda. That was all it had taken to send Felix scrambling away from a new and important client. His mind whirled as he raced across town, breaking every traffic law. He couldn't get to Koda fast enough. At the hospital, he had shown his ID and been redirected three times before he finally found the right room. Nothing in his life had prepared him for the sight that met him.

It was like a war zone. There were surgical supplies littering every surface. Blood streaked the floor and several wadded-up clothes. The room felt devoid of life. Machines scattered around an empty bed. Koda sat quietly in the corner. Tears streaked his pale face. Felix crossed the room, moving slowly as the shock tried chattering his teeth. He locked his jaw against the sensation. Felix had never seen anyone more broken than Koda. He looked as if he had witnessed a living nightmare and would never be the same. It wasn't until he got closer that Felix noticed Koda's shirt was open and there was a tiny baby cradled against his skin, sharing Koda's warmth.

"Hey, baby."

Koda's face turned his way at Felix's softly spoken greeting. His expression crumbled. "He has ten of the tiniest fingers and toes. I counted."

Felix collapsed into the chair beside Koda when his knees refused to keep holding him. He draped his arm across the back of Koda's chair and inspected the pink ball against Koda's chest. He was so small, Felix could barely see him beyond his blue knit hat. There was a tiny ID bracelet around his ankle. It matched the one Koda wore around his wrist. Felix tried comforting Koda.

. . .

"It's okay, baby. I'm here."

Koda took a stuttered breath. "He's ours. They fought, but..." Koda's voice broke.

Felix's eyes filled with tears. Since the day Megan had shown up at his studio and asked this of them, Felix had made a point of avoiding her. He had shown up to all the lawyer's appointments and signed everything he had been asked to sign. But Felix had been bitter. Megan had cheated and ruined his life. She had tried to take him for everything in their divorce, and the love they once shared had turned to hatred. Felix had loved her enough to marry her once. He couldn't believe she was gone, and the thing that had driven them apart now connected them forever.

Felix pushed aside Koda's shirt and took a better look at their son. Even with tears blurring his vision, Felix could see that he was perfect. "So, this is Liam, huh?" He tried hard not to sound as shattered as he felt. "He's beautiful."

. . .

Koda cried harder.

Felix pulled his two babies against his chest and held on. He tried holding Koda tighter without squishing Liam. "We'll be okay. We'll make sure he knows how much his mom loved him."

"She died for this," Koda whispered against his chest. "He's so perfect. I didn't expect to love him, but I do. I don't know how to feel. It's not fair."

"We'll figure everything out together, but I think Megan would still want us to celebrate his life the way people would any birth. This is what she asked of us."

"Okay, Dad number two. I have an ID ready for you too." Felix's head jerked up as a nurse walked in and chatted like this was a normal day. "These bracelets have alarms in them connected to baby Liam's bracelet. That way no one can walk out with your baby. Let's get this on you."

Felix dutifully held out his wrist.

She snapped it closed. "Hospital policy is that at least one parent stay overnight with the new baby to prove you can care for him before leaving. Which of you will be staying with us?"

"I'll stay," Felix said without having to think about it. Koda had been through enough for one day.

"We'll both stay," Koda said, correcting him as he wiped his eyes.

The woman looked between them. Her expression looked pinched, proving she wasn't as oblivious to their pain as she pretended. "I've got a room set up for you. Do you have him, Dad? Or would you like for me to carry him?"

. . .

Koda shook his head and stood, being careful to keep Liam bundled against his chest. "I've got him."

Felix set his hand on the small of Koda's back and steered him through the mess. He tried not to look at the empty bed as they passed or the blood-soaked bedding. They headed down the hall and into a clean room. A clear bassinet and diaper bag stuffed with essentials waited along with a hospital bed and chair. Felix led Koda to the chair.

"All right, Dads. Who wants to change the first diaper?"

Felix still hadn't recovered from the shock of Megan's death, and the world kept spinning like nothing happened. He was tossed onto a moving train he knew nothing about. The thing was, though, he loved Koda, and that was what saved him from drowning. Koda was devastated, and Felix knew how to be a good husband. That rescued him now. "I'll do it."

Felix took the baby from Koda, making sure he supported his head as he moved to the bassinet. The nurse gave him pointers and Felix survived his first diaper change and swaddle by soldiering through. Next, she taught him how to make a bottle and told him about Liam's feeding schedule. They talked about who Liam's pediatrician would be while Felix settled on the bed and fed Liam. Liam's dark eyes opened and latched on to Felix while he ate. Felix's heart stopped and time slipped away. He swore Liam knew that he belonged to Felix now. Felix realized his heart belonged to Liam too. He toyed with Liam's tiny fingers and something inside him grew. This was his son. He was helpless without Felix and Koda. Liam couldn't survive without them.

"You're so quiet."

. . .

Felix glanced Koda's way at the softly spoken words. His mouth opened and spilled all his secrets. "You're right. He's perfect."

"We're so unprepared for this."

Despite the horror of the day, light found its way in and a chuckle escaped Felix. "Just call your mom. I imagine we have nothing to worry about. She'll have us completely sorted before we get home."

A small smile touched Koda's lips. It fell away as quickly as it appeared. "We shouldn't have pretended this wouldn't happen." Another shaky breath escaped Koda. "I was just laughing with her less than two hours ago. Now she's gone and we're parents."

Felix's gaze moved back to Liam. He was asleep with the bottle still in his mouth. Felix wished he knew what to say to make everything better. He knew that wasn't possible, but he also knew in his heart this little guy had the magic power of healing. Liam made Felix feel less horrible. "Do you want to hold him some more?"

Another tear slipped down Koda's face. "I really do."

Felix stood and placed Liam in Koda's waiting arms. As he stared at the pair, love filled him to overflowing. It had been a horrible and tragic day, but Felix felt like they would be okay. He had never dreamed he could love anything or anyone at just one glance. This baby proved that wasn't true. He hadn't wanted Liam. Felix had wanted Megan to survive and raise her child. But now Liam was his, and Felix wanted this family that had fallen into his lap. Koda looked like he should have a baby in his arms. Felix's throat swelled. They didn't know the first thing about being parents, but they would learn. They would make Megan proud. Liam would always be loved. Felix would guarantee it.

TEN

MUSIC BLARED THROUGH THE BACKYARD. Water splashed in the pool. Bright car-shaped balloons were tied to every surface, making Zayn wonder if a strong gust would carry the entire yard away. The birthday boy, Liam, squished cake on his highchair, happy to be the center of attention. While everyone oohed and aahed over the freshly turned one-year-old, Zayn couldn't tear his gaze away from the DJ.

Once again, Zealous Blaze aka Spencer Wright had volunteered to make the party a gathering no one would forget. Since Zayn had first set eyes on Spencer at Koda and Felix's wedding, he had become a tad bit obsessed with the uber famous DJ. He reminded Zayn of a Viking. His light blond hair and beard caught the eye, but that was easy since he stood nearly a foot taller than everyone else. With headphones covering his ears, Spencer moved to the beat of the music while avoiding everyone's stares. It was like he was lost in the music, or maybe he just didn't like anyone. Either way, Zayn felt an overwhelming desire to meet Spencer's stare.

As if Spencer felt him watching, Spencer's chin lifted. His ice-blue gaze skirted the crowd until it landed on Zayn. His mouth lifted in one corner into a sexy smirk before his gaze moved back to his task. Zayn lost his breath. He had met tons of celebrities over the years. Zayn couldn't count the number of people he had been introduced to who were way more well known than Spencer. He couldn't explain the draw, but he wanted this guy. This one. It was a fire in his gut.

Someone slapped him across the back, startling him from his torment. Felix flashed him a bright smile as

Zayn looked his way. "I should introduce you to Spencer. You didn't get to meet him at the wedding."

As Felix steered Zayn closer to Spencer, he tried to stay calm. He felt like he was headed toward his destiny. It would either be a disaster, or it wouldn't. He was completely ready to get his life leveled, if it meant he got a shot at Spencer. Bring on the pain.

As always, Koda's mom had gone way overboard for a baby's birthday party. Poor Liam would be a terror later, after all the sugar. By his mom's descriptions, Koda gathered that Liam was covered head to toe in cake. Luckily, she had promised to clean up the mess and babysit if he was climbing the walls later. Koda kind of hoped it happened. While unexpectedly becoming a parent had been a wild and amazing ride, Koda missed having Felix to himself sometimes.

As if Felix felt Koda's longing for him, his arm encircled Koda's waist, towing him back against the body Koda loved. Felix's lips touched the shell of

Koda's ear. "Your mom has everything under control. You should join me inside."

Butterflies stirred in Koda's stomach. "Is that so?"

Felix kissed his neck. "Definitely."

Goosebumps rose on Koda's skin. It had been so long since they made love. They were always rushed or hiding to steal quick moments alone. Koda missed the intimacy. Felix took Koda's hand and led him inside. It wasn't until Felix headed up the stairs that Koda's curiosity hit an all-time high.

"What's going on?"

A sexy chuckle caressed Koda's ears. "Your mom is about to give Liam a bath and his party is winding down." Felix led Koda into a spare bedroom and Koda heard the door close behind them. "I don't know if you realize it, since life has been hectic, but as of last week, we've been together two years."

Koda did some quick math in his head. "Huh. Where did time go?"

Felix moved Koda across the room until he was sitting on the edge of the bed. "Your mom plans to keep Liam and Rachel's kids tonight so we can finally head to the beach to scatter Megan's ashes." At the mention of Megan, Koda's throat automatically swelled. Since her death, they had taken Liam to North Carolina a few times so he could visit his aunt and cousins. This was the first time they had flown Rachel to California. It was well past the time they should finally fulfill Megan's last wishes. Still, her sacrifice was never far from Koda's mind. He never forgot what he gained from her loss.

"That's probably a good idea. It's well past time for us to do that."

. . .

Felix ran his thumb across Koda's bottom lip, pulling him away from his depressing thoughts. "I was thinking, tomorrow, after we take Rachel to the airport, maybe we could head out to Santa Barbara again. We could stay in your favorites bungalows and introduce Liam to our spot."

A smile snapped to Koda's lips. "I would love that. You still haven't explained why we're hiding in the guest room."

Felix pushed, toppling Koda onto his back before straddling his body. "We haven't been alone in a while."

Koda's body stirred as Felix's lips brushed his. "I'm aware." Even to Koda's ears, he sounded breathless.

"I told your mom where we would be if Liam needs us. Otherwise, she promised we wouldn't be disturbed."

. . .

At Felix's claim, Koda embraced his growing desire. He ran his hands up Felix's back, pulling Felix's shirt up as he went. "Is that so?"

Felix nuzzled Koda's neck. "Yep. I have you all to myself."

"What do you plan to do with me?"

Felix unbuttoned Koda's jeans. "First, I plan to make love to you and then I want to hold you while you take a long nap."

Damn. That sounded like heaven. First, Koda had something to say. He flattened his palms against Felix's shoulders to make him pay attention. "The past two years with you have been the best of my life. I'm proud you're my husband and you're the best dad on the planet. You're also my best friend. Every time I think I can't love you more, I do."

. . .

Felix released a stuttered-sounding breath. "It's like you read my thoughts and said them back to me. We've had a lot of things thrown our way, and there's not a single person on this planet I would've rather faced them with than you. You're my person."

"Forever."

Felix's hand slipped inside Koda's jeans. "Exactly. Don't you ever forget it."

Koda's cheeks hurt, making him realize how big his smile had grown. He couldn't imagine life with anyone else. His smile slipped away and turned to moans as Felix stroked him exactly the way he liked. Two years ago, Koda never could have predicted this future. Now he would kill to keep this life. He knew love like he had never felt before. Koda saw their future, and it was perfect. They would grow old together and raise a good man together. Felix and Koda would always lean on each other and face every battle while holding hands. They had made mistakes over the years while trying to find each other and been blind to each other's existence. Those days were behind them now. They were real and solid. Beautiful. They were each other's happy ending.

———

While Felix hadn't planned to seduce his husband at his in-law's house, he had no plans to stop. Unfortunately, since he hadn't planned to seduce his husband, he wasn't prepared for anything penetrating. He wouldn't risk hurting Koda and ruining their night alone. Thank god for Elena. Felix loved his son more than life, but he needed a night alone with Koda.

Felix still had his pants hanging off one leg and Koda had barely gotten his jeans pushed down his hips before Felix straddled him, grabbed their cocks, and stroked. With his forehead pressed to Koda's, he moved against him. It wasn't sexy. He didn't have any porn moves. But they were connected and beautiful. He could feel Koda's love and he did his best to make Koda feel his too. He burned for Koda every second of the day. Time strengthened his feelings every day. He never tired of dedicating his life to this. Felix adored this man.

His muscles clenched much faster than he liked. He tried holding out, but he couldn't get enough of Koda. His mind knew he was making love to the sexiest man alive. There was no staving off the pleasure. Koda dug his fingernails into Felix's shoulders and gasped. Hot cum poured over Felix's fingers, snapping his brain. Felix thrust faster against his palm. He didn't fight the building orgasm. When the first spasm hit, Koda's name fell from Felix's lips. Koda claimed his mouth like he hoped to taste Felix crying out for him.

Felix's mind was a mess as he massaged out every drop of cum, stealing every moment of ecstasy. They whispered their love as Felix moved away to grab a washcloth from the bathroom. He stripped and cleaned himself before bringing a warm, wet cloth back for Koda. Koda was nude and waiting. Felix drew a steady breath in through his nose as he cleaned Koda's skin. He kissed Koda's freshly washed stomach.

. . .

"You're gorgeous. I never get enough of looking at you."

A sexy and tired-sounding chuckle caressed Felix's ears. Koda ran his fingers through Felix's hair. "You're such a flatterer, but I know the truth. Gabby says I'm getting fat and staying home with Liam has caused me to lose my sense of style."

"Gabby can get fucked." Seriously, Felix couldn't stand that bitter old lady. "You're perfect and anyone who says otherwise is a complete dumbass."

Koda didn't stop smiling. "I think you're a bit biased."

Felix kissed Koda's chest before rolling to one side and spooning Koda. "I don't know. All I know is that I would choose you every day, even if I woke up every day having to start over. I wouldn't change a thing about you. Every time I look at you, I want to shove you into the nearest closet and fuck you. That feeling never goes away."

Koda's body shook with barely suppressed laughter. "I love you."

"I love you too," Felix said against Koda's temple. "You're my entire world." Felix had never meant anything more. The past two years with Koda had taken him on a whirlwind journey. Felix had discovered so much about himself. He learned how to forgive Megan and himself for their stubborn inability to lean on each other. Felix had regained his love for her in a new way. Every day, they let Liam know she loved him and would be so proud of him. Each and every day, Felix watched Koda with their son and he fell deeper in love than he had ever been in his life. He recognized that his crazy passion for hanging on to relationships had only been practice for Koda. Everything had been leading him here to this life. This man. He wouldn't take a second for granted. Nothing was ever guaranteed. But Felix would love Koda and Liam to his dying breath, and god willing, he would find Koda in the next life too. No amount of lifetimes would ever be enough.

Keep an eye out for the next Candied Crush, *Beautifully Spun*.

Please consider leaving a review at the retailer where you purchased this book. Reviews really help with a book's visibility, which allows me to continue writing more stories. Thank you, Charity.

ABOUT THE AUTHOR

Charity Parkerson is an award-winning and multi-published author with several companies. Born with no filter from her brain to her mouth, she decided to take this odd quirk and insert it in her characters.

*Eight-time Readers' Favorite Award Winner
    *2015 Passionate Plume Award Finalist
    *2013 Reviewers' Choice Award Winner
    *2012 ARRA Finalist for Favorite Paranormal Romance
    *Five-time winner of The Mistress of the Darkpath

Connect with her online:

—Sign up for my newsletter: https://sendfox.com/charityparkerson
    —Join my readers' group on Facebook: http://bit.ly/CharitysTribe
    —Website: charityparkerson.com

—Facebook: facebook.com/authorCharityParkerson

facebook.com/TheMenofSin

—Twitter: twitter.com/CharityParkerso

—Instagram: Instagram.com/sinnerauthor

—Bookbub: https://www.bookbub.com/authors/charity-parkerson

—Amazon page: author.to/CharityParkerson

—TikTok: http://www.tiktok.com/@charityparkerson